DIRT NAP

Other Bella Books by Carolyn Elizabeth

Gallows Humor

About the Author

Carolyn Elizabeth is an enthusiastic writer of romantic lesbian fiction where serious camp meets upbeat macabre.

She was born in Canada and moved to the US as a young child. She has lived in Illinois, New York, New Hampshire, Texas, Maryland, and Connecticut before moving back to Canada in 2013.

She lives with her family in London, Ontario where she has parlayed her education and professional experience in pathology into a satisfying job in tissue banking for cancer research.

When not working or writing, she can be found goofing around with her children, cuddling with the dogs while binge watching Netflix, and taking afternoons off work to have adult lunch dates with her wife.

DIRT NAP

Carolyn Elizabeth

BELLA
B O O K S
2020

Bella Books, Inc.
P.O. Box 10543
Tallahassee, FL 32302

Printed in the United States of America on acid-free paper.

First Bella Books Edition 2020

Editor: Ann Roberts
Cover Designer: Judith Fellows

ISBN: 978-1-64247-102-1

Acknowledgments

Endless thanks to the Bella Books family for all they do to support authors and get our work out there into the world. Thank you to Ann Roberts for taking on the herculean task of editing another one of my books. I'll read a manual on punctuation for dialogue before the next one—wait, I mean the one after. I promise.

Thank you to the readers and reviewers whose thoughtful, insightful, and critical comments help inspire and motivate me in new ways with every project.

Thank you to my wife, Laurel, for her continued encouragement and her willingness to laugh, not just with me, but at me.

As ever, to my children, Henry and Grayson, thank you for helping me grow into my best possible person—and my most patient.

CHAPTER ONE

Corey Curtis turned up the volume to Joan Jett's "Crimson and Clover" and drummed on the steering wheel of her vintage Ford F-100 as she drove away from the hospital. A trip into the field and away from her basement office in the morgue was always welcome, especially in nice weather. Her mood soared and she fought laughter, although she was on her way to a crime scene and the recovery of a partially decomposed body.

It was a hot, breezy, late August day in Jackson City, New York, in the Southern Tier, and for the first time in thirty-three years, she was in love—madly, deeply, insanely in love with Dr. Thayer Reynolds, a woman so wonderful and beautiful that when Corey looked at her, she thought her heart would beat right out of her chest. She wanted to jump up and down on Oprah's couch and scream at the top of her lungs.

She was downright giddy at finally having the use of both hands after seven weeks in a full cast on her left arm. She had sustained a broken arm and other serious injuries in a freak attack from a murderer. She and Thayer had inadvertently solved a crime while snooping around the construction site where the foreman had died after a five-story fall, a fall Corey had always believed was suspicious.

A deep breath at the memory triggered the tolerable ache just beneath her left breast from the three broken ribs she suffered. She still had some healing to do. She rolled her shoulders and neck, loosening the muscles damaged when she fought the man in defense of herself and Thayer. She beat him, knocking him out, only to fall fifteen feet through an unfinished floor, and Thayer, unable to help, had watched it happen.

Broken bones and internal injuries weren't even her biggest concern compared to the massive concussion and the debilitating headaches she still endured almost two months out from the accident. The migraines occurred less often and didn't always require medication any longer, but they still incapacitated her for the better part of a day.

She shook herself out of her melancholy thoughts and adjusted the specially tinted glasses that protected her from UV and fluorescent light, the constant insult of which frequently triggered an attack. She focused on the day ahead and the recovery of the dead body.

Dr. Audrey Marsh, the forensic anthropologist at the university and Corey's former mentor as an undergraduate, had been called by the police to assist on a case. At one time Corey had dreamed of a career in forensic anthropology but was seduced away by a master's degree in pathology as a certified pathologists' assistant. She could now boast a decent paycheck with good benefits and the position of Autopsy Services Coordinator at Jackson City Memorial Hospital. She had worked there for the last five years, overseeing the post mortem examinations under the supervision of Dr. Randall Webster, the forensic pathologist.

Still, she kept in touch with Dr. Marsh and was involved in forensic cases as they came up and overlapped with her work. She hadn't assisted with a forensic case in a while and was far more excited than even she would have thought, given the gruesome death scene that awaited them at their destination. If the body was so far gone they needed Dr. Marsh's help, it was going to be nothing but horrible.

She looked over at Cinnamon James riding shotgun. Cin was Dr. Marsh's student, Corey's friend and sometimes assistant. "Look Mom, two hands," Corey blurted gleefully, her hands at ten and two on the wheel.

Cin smiled at her before returning to her phone. "You're spirited today."

"I told Thayer I'm in love with her this morning."

Cin held her phone up to get a better satellite signal. "That comes as a surprise to exactly no one."

"Well, sure, okay." Corey shrugged, still grinning. "But I said it out loud and I just feel like...I don't know. I feel like everything's changed."

Cin nodded. "God, my phone sucks."

Corey pulled her much newer phone from her back pocket. "Here."

"What did she say?" Cin asked.

"She said 'I know.'"

"What the hell does that mean?"

Corey slanted her an incredulous glance. Cin was frighteningly bright and accomplished, well on her way to a PhD in forensic anthropology at Jackson City University, and Corey often forgot she was nearly ten years younger. Still, Corey wasn't born yet when the movie Thayer quoted was released so that was no excuse. "From *The Empire Strikes Back.* Han to Leia after she confesses her love right before he's frozen in carbonite."

"Was Natalie Portman in that one?"

"What? Never mind." She came to a stop at Main Street. "Which way?"

"West. Looks like we're heading down Old South Road to Rankins Lake."

Corey's head whipped toward her. "Where?"

"Um." Cin studied the directions as they continued through what passed for the business district in the small city of just over sixty-three thousand people. "Looks like the north side—Corey, stop!" she screamed as she looked up and threw her arm toward the dash.

Corey's eyes snapped back to the road and she stood on the brakes, slamming them against their seat belts as the truck screeched to within inches of the car in front of them. Corey threw her arm out across Cin in the passenger seat. "Oh, fuck."

"Jesus Christ, Corey," Cin panted, dropping her head back against her seat and pulling at her belt that had tightened across her.

"Shit." Corey's heart pounded. She met the wide-eyed stare of the other driver in his rearview mirror and offered an apologetic wave. He took off as soon as the light turned green, apparently wanting to put as much distance between them as possible. "Are you all right?"

"Yeah." Cin rubbed her collarbone where the belt had dug in.

"Oh, shit, I'm sorry." Corey winced at her reddening skin.

"Are you getting a headache or something?"

"No," Corey said and started moving when the car behind her honked. "Thayer lives on Rankins Lake and just for a second..."

"Yeah, I know. So do other people, Corey. And didn't you just see Thayer at work, like an hour ago?"

"Yeah, I know it's stupid." Corey smiled sheepishly. "I'm sorry. I just flaked out for a second."

"Do I need to drive?" Cin offered her a smile in apparent acceptance of her apology. "So you can be alone with your distracting thoughts?"

"I got it." Corey shook her head, focusing on the road. "Just tell me where we're going."

CHAPTER TWO

They turned off Old South Road onto a smaller, unnamed access road half a mile from Thayer's place and began winding their way around to the opposite side of the lake. The road narrowed, going from paved to gravel to dirt, and closed in by dense trees and ground foliage.

Corey squinted through the windshield, sunlight strobing in through the trees as they bumped along slowly. She couldn't help wincing as the jostling and light flashes caused her some discomfort. "How much farther?"

"Almost." Cin peered up ahead. "There." She pointed to the patrol car pulled off in the brush, marking a drive of little more than two rutted dirt tracks heading toward the lake.

Corey stopped as a young officer held out his hand. He was her height, muscular arms straining against his shirtsleeves with closely cropped brown hair that glistened with sweat beneath his uniform cap. She didn't recognize him but couldn't fail to notice his sickly pallor and sweaty skin. As soon as she rolled the window down, she got blasted by the hot, fetid stench that could only be putrefying tissue. "Corey Curtis and Cinnamon James." She held up her hospital ID badge and breathed through her mouth. "They're expecting us."

The officer swallowed heavily several times in an effort to speak, but in the end decided keeping his mouth closed was the safer option and simply waved them forward.

Corey's face lit up at the sight of Audrey Marsh leaning against her battered Corolla, lighting a cigarette from the butt of one she'd just finished. Corey knew it was her recovery car and she drove a Benz on campus. Though it had been at least a year since Corey had seen her last at a lecture she had given, she hadn't changed at all. She was small, five-foot-three, with wiry muscled arms and legs. She still wore no jewelry and no makeup, her almost completely gray hair in a long single braid down her back.

She waved, blowing a stream of smoke through her nose as Corey and Cin parked next to the ambulance. Two miserable-looking paramedics huddled in the cab, using the tails of their shirts to cover their noses.

Corey jumped out fast and slammed the door in a futile effort to keep the air in the truck clean. Her eyes watered and she coughed at the overpowering miasma of human decomposition. Her eyes tracked to the house, an old rundown double-wide with busted screens, mold on the siding, and a roof she was certain leaked in at least three places.

At the front of the house, to the right of rickety wooden porch steps, a section of rotting latticework had been pulled out and set aside revealing the entrance to a crawlspace beneath the house. The mouth of the pit was completely dark but the drone of the flies was so loud she could hear it from where she stood, and there was a cloud of flies at the entrance buzzing in and out.

"Corey." Audrey Marsh's voice was smoker's rough as she pinched out her cigarette and pocketed the butt. "It's good to see you." She pulled Corey into a much stronger hug than her size suggested.

"Dr. Marsh, how are you?"

"Corey, I'm not going to tell you again about calling me Audrey. How long has it been since you were my student? Ten years? We're colleagues."

"Twelve."

"Damn that makes me feel old." Audrey sighed and lit another cigarette as she eyed her former student. "Are you up for this? Cin told me everything."

"I'm much better Dr. Mar—um, Audrey," Corey stammered, trying out her first name. "I've been cleared for work."

Audrey nodded and took a long drag. "I wanted to come see you in the hospital but I was at conferences all summer. I only just got back before Webster and the police started blowing up my phone. I haven't even unpacked."

"It's okay. Cin told me you were out of the country, and besides, I wasn't very good company for a while."

"Hmm." Audrey took a long drag. "I hear you made a friend over the summer?"

Corey couldn't help the grin that split her face at the mention of Thayer.

Audrey laughed and gripped her arms. "Love looks good on you, my young friend." She took a final drag before pinching it out, her expression turning serious. "I'm glad you're here today."

Corey grimaced, acutely aware that they were chatting in very close proximity to an unidentified and rapidly decomposing body they were tasked with extricating from a very dark, very hot, and very small resting place. "I was pretty excited until I opened the car door."

"I've done an awful lot of recoveries in my time, and you never really get used to it, but even I think this one will be rough." Her eyes trained on the opening to the crawlspace.

Talking about it brought the stench to the forefront of Corey's mind again and she coughed. "Hope you brought some gel."

"Always." Audrey produced a small jar of mentholated gel from her pocket, unscrewed the lid and dug her finger in. She swiped a glob beneath her nose and offered it to Corey. "It's why I'll never knock off the smoking. Nasty habit but kills the respiratory cilia."

Corey did the same, smearing it under her nose to cut the foul air. "I better check in with Collier and get dressed."

Audrey barked a laugh. "He's as fun as ever." She popped the trunk of her car to get her equipment. "See you in the trenches."

Corey headed over to Jim Collier, who was looking especially disheveled with his tie loosened and his shirtsleeves rolled up. He was imposing at well over six feet tall with cropped graying hair and a gruff voice and demeanor. He was a sergeant with the Jackson City Police Department and they had often worked together when he was assigned cases that involved her postmortem exams. They had always had a friendly relationship, but since Corey's injuries from her involvement in the previous case, they had begun to realize they were friends.

Today he stood with an unfamiliar female patrol officer, thumbs hooked into her duty belt and head on a swivel, her eyes hidden behind her aviators. She looked to be a few inches shorter than Corey, maybe five-foot-seven. She was powerfully built but still feminine even in the shapeless uniform and Kevlar vest.

Collier nodded between them as he scribbled in his ever-present notebook, which was like an extension of his hand. "Curtis, Austin. Austin, Curtis."

Corey shook her head disapprovingly and extended her hand. "Corey."

"Steph."

Collier glanced at Corey briefly. "You look different."

She waved her left arm. "Got my cast off this morning."

He grunted and coughed. "Just in time. I'd go down with you but it's a tight fit."

"My ass you would," Corey shot back, noticing the twitch of a smile from Steph Austin. "I'm going to get set." She headed back to her truck and Steph joined her.

Corey was already impressed with her. The air was so foul with decay you could taste it, and if Officer Steph Austin was bothered by it, she gave no indication. Maybe she was anosmic and couldn't smell. "I can tell just by the way you stand that you've been doing this a while. You pull the short straw to get this gig?" she asked as she dropped the tailgate.

Steph seemed pleased with Corey's comment. "I'm coming up on twenty years. I'm partnered with Sergeant Collier for the time being."

"You could do a hell of a lot worse."

"And I have," Steph agreed, staring at Corey's vivid, full sleeve, ocean life tattoo on her right arm. "That looks like Frankie Fortune's work."

"You know Frankie?"

Steph's mouth quirked. "Maybe."

Corey's eyes narrowed and she assessed the woman again. The only skin that was showing was from the neck up and her arms in her summer uniform.

"You'll never guess and I'm not the tramp stamp type of girl," Steph deadpanned.

Corey laughed. She really liked Steph Austin and could see them being friends. "So, how long are you going to be riding with Collier?"

"Unknown at this time, but you'll be seeing me around as long as I am."

"Where he goes you go?"

"Pretty much." Steph grimaced and removed her sunglasses. "In this case, though, I'm going with you. Photos and evidence."

"What? In there?"

Steph smiled and now Corey could see the lines around her hazel eyes. There were more than a few strands of gray streaking through her brown hair pulled into a bun at the nape of her neck. She was older than Corey originally thought, and if she'd been on the job for twenty years, she was at least in her early forties. She looked more than physically capable. "Are you sure about that?"

"Absolutely not but it's the job."

"Atta girl. Let's get you kitted out. What are you wearing under your uniform?"

Steph cocked a brow at her. "I have a T-shirt on if that's what you mean."

"It is." Corey smiled. "Take your vest, duty belt and uniform top off. Don't wear anything that could get caught and tear your suit, and don't bring anything you would have to go back in for if you lost. The suits are thin so empty your pockets." She patted the Tyvek suit. "It's also going to be hot as hell in there so the less you have on the better." Corey scanned the contents of her truck bed. "Oh, shit, I forgot to pick up water."

"The patrol cars have bottles in the trunk. They'll be warm but I'll make sure we get some."

"Great. All of it. We're going to need it. Get the suit on and I'll help you with the rest. And if you have to pee do it now."

"Right." Steph took the suit and headed to Collier's unmarked car to take her gear off, and he, in turn, wandered over to Corey's truck.

"I like your partner," Corey said to him as she stepped into her own suit.

"Who? Stone Cold?" He snorted as he continued writing whatever he was writing in the little notebook.

"Why do you call her that?" Corey glanced at him while she exchanged her expensive glasses for a pair of hardware store, yellow-tinted safety glasses. They didn't work as well long term but were fine for short periods, and she wasn't risking her good ones. Then she pulled thick, disposable boots over her shoes and tied them up over her calves.

"She's a goddamn robot—totally emotionless. Never talks about herself. Never cracks a smile. Don't even know if she's gay or straight."

"What the hell difference does that make to how well she does her job?"

"It doesn't. I just mean no one knows anything about her."

"Maybe because a woman in the good old boy police force feels like she can't emote lest it be used against her in some way."

He eyed her over his notes. "Like what way?"

"Like being called a bitch, a dyke, or a tease. Your nickname? Stone Cold Steph Austin—very clever, by the way—already screams, 'You should smile more, honey, you'll be prettier.'"

Collier grunted and turned back to his notes. "I didn't make it up and she's not my partner. She's training. The brass are grooming her for advancement. Some initiative from the mayor's office to promote more women into leadership."

"Oh, I see. It's because she's a woman and not because she's put in twenty years in a uniform with an impeccable service record, and she probably aced the detective's exam and has still been passed over for promotion repeatedly?"

He snapped his notebook closed and glared at her. "What do you know about it? She tell you all that?"

Corey snorted and snapped her first layer of gloves over her hands. "Nope. Didn't have to. I know how it works."

"It's not my fault there are hardly any women on the force."

"Oh, really? Because the police have such a strong history of recruiting and welcoming women?"

"The fitness requirements are strict and it's a dangerous profession. Women are—"

"Do not finish that sentence. I like and respect you, Collier, but I think I hate you a little bit right now." She pulled on heavier weight gloves and pulled them up her wrists as far as they would go. "Do you even hear the bullshit coming out of your mouth right now?"

"I'm not sexist," he barked. "You know me."

Corey rolled her eyes. "Oh, I'm sorry. That's right, hashtag not all men. Well, what are you doing to change the culture? How many of your bros in blue have you told to shut the fuck up when you hear them spouting filth about pussy grabbing in the locker room?"

He looked away. "I'm not going to win this, am I?"

"Nope. Don't worry, Collier. I know you're one of the good guys. When we finish this case, I'll take you out for a beer and introduce you to terms like 'toxic masculinity' and 'mansplaining.'"

"Man—what?"

From behind them Steph Austin coughed to cover a laugh, drawing their attention, but couldn't contain the bright smile lighting up her face letting Corey know she had most likely heard much of their conversation.

Corey grinned knowingly and threw her a wink, admitting Steph Austin was quite attractive when she smiled. Corey immediately quelled the thought and turned her attention back to the job at hand. Steph had the department-issued camera and was tasked with taking the photos of the body and scene under the house, as well as recovering any obvious evidence before the crime scene unit came to do a more thorough sweep once the body was out. Of course, they risked contaminating the scene by going in first, but the only way around that would be to move the house to allow proper access. An expense like that would be astronomical and would never be approved by the city.

Corey helped Steph with her gloves, booties, and respirator mask. She gave her a pair of safety glasses and a face shield that would go on last after they pulled the suit hoods up and snugged the elastic around their faces. Their personal protective equipment would do as much to protect the scene from them as it would protect them from the scene.

She glanced to the entrance as Cin and Audrey were setting down the battery powered portable LED lights, a backboard from the ambulance, a heavy-duty black body bag and a stack of towels.

"Looks like we're set." She looked at Steph. "Ready?"

"No."

CHAPTER THREE

"You and Sergeant Collier pretty good friends?" Steph asked.

"I guess." Corey was already sweating and breathing heavily, her skin itching beneath the suit. She was grateful for idle conversation and something else to think about. "In our line of work we cross paths a lot. We've been colleagues for five years or so. The friends part came about a little more recently. Why do you ask?"

"He respects you a great deal. Cares about you and what you think."

"There's no way he told you that." She laughed. "We go out of our way to never say nice things to or about one another— kind of like siblings."

"He didn't," Steph agreed. "I just know I've never heard anyone bust his balls the way you just did and live to tell."

"Yeah." Corey grinned. "That was fun. He needed to hear it."

"You respect him?"

Corey could tell that despite her casual tone, she was fishing. "Very much. He's a great cop and I would trust him with my life. Nearly had to just recently, in fact."

"I'm familiar with your story. What you did was really…"

"Please, don't say brave."

"I was going to say stupid, but we just met and I wasn't sure how that would go over."

She laughed. "I can live with that. Probably the only time Collier's said nice things to me or called me by my first name was when I was in the hospital. His mouth may say differently sometimes but his heart is always in the right place. A little rough around the edges but he's a great guy."

"I think so too," Steph said quietly.

"Yeah?" There was an almost imperceptible wistfulness in her tone and Corey glanced at her.

"If you ever repeat that to him they will never find your body." Her voice was cool as ice but the glint in her eyes belied her threat.

"Understood."

The four women stood garbed head to toe in protective plastic and nitrile just outside the range of the green bottle fly swarm.

"Can you fill us in, Steph?" Corey asked.

"Nothing about the body," Cin added.

Audrey nodded. "Any information or suspicions about cause of death might prejudice our analysis."

"No worries there." Steph coughed. "We don't know a thing. Not even sex. Early this morning a couple of hikers caught the stench, and thinking it was a dead animal, decided to investigate. When they realized the house was the origin they went no further and called 911. A patrol car came out and made the discovery. He only poked his head and flashlight in far enough to determine a human body."

"That the poor guy out on the road?" Corey asked.

"Yeah. Officer Kelly Warren. On the job six years. This is his first body discovery. The sergeant and I did a sweep of the interior and immediate grounds to determine there were no other deceased, injured or other immediate threats and called you. The crime scene unit is standing by until after the recovery."

"Good enough," Audrey replied, taking charge. "Corey, I want you to go in first and set up the lights. Do your best not to interfere with the scene. We have no idea yet how much room we'll have and your height makes you the limiting factor, so get your bearings and let us know. Officer Austin is in next to get her photos and whatever else she needs. If it's too crowded, one of the two of you will pop back out, and we'll send the backboard and bag in. We're going to roll the body and bag it in there to avoid causing any more damage on the way out. The backboard will keep the body from flopping around. We can pack it with towels on the outside to sop up the mess." She held out the tin of gel. "Last chance."

Everyone dug in and smeared the gel over their faces before affixing their masks in place and lowering their face shields.

Corey did her best to ignore the flies and stepped down into the hole. So far it was only two feet deep and she peered down seeing it dropped further. "I'm good." She hunkered down and folded herself into the gap, her chest and back muscles informing her of their displeasure.

She was in and felt for the bottom of the house, touching the ceiling of the crawlspace easily from her knees. "About four feet high." She leaned back out. "Pass me the lights."

Cin handed them down one at a time. "You okay?"

Corey coughed. "Great. Let's make this quick."

She ducked back down, breathing heavily through her mask. The heat was oppressive and made even heavier by the indescribable sickening stench. Her scrubs stuck to her back and legs, and sweat prickled against her scalp and trickled down her face beneath her glasses and mask. There was no way she could brush it away so she endured.

She didn't want to move too far into the crawlspace for fear of stumbling over the body. She would have liked to prepare more, but she couldn't spend any longer than necessary. The respirator protected them from biohazard particles but did nothing to cut the smell, which was so dense she imagined she could see it. She flicked on the first light, blinking against the visual assault.

The scene revealed was so gruesome that her breath was stolen, and a cry of alarm was impossible. The body, unclothed but for boots and socks lay along the far wall from where she knelt—a writhing, undulating mass of insect activity. The maggots carpeted the face and neck and part of the torso and groin. Their movement made a wet, popping sound as they fed and grew. "Dear god."

Corey set up the other lights against the walls in a quadrant as fast as she could, doing her best to avoid the ground immediately around the body. She estimated the space at fifteen feet square—a tight squeeze for all of them. She didn't want to be alone any longer. "Steph?" She gagged and choked back bile.

Corey moved farther back as Steph hunched in. "Jesus Christ." Steph choked, her eyes going enormously wide through the shield.

Corey patted her hard on the shoulder. "I know. Get the job done," she managed, and to Steph's credit, she immediately began snapping her photos and studying the ground for any evidence, gently sifting through the dirt with her fingers.

"It's tight but we can make it work. Send in the backboard and bag and come down," Corey directed to the anxiously peering eyes of Audrey and Cin.

She set the backboard out of the way and arranged the body bag so it was open and ready to receive its cargo, leaving room for Audrey and Cin.

Steph clicked away on the camera, but all Corey could hear was the sound of her own labored, nearly panicked breathing. No one deserved to be found like this.

"Holy Mary. That poor bastard," Audrey said while Cin went pale and silent at the sight of the rotting, bug-infested corpse. They had no reason to know it was a man save the body was large, despite the decay.

"You have everything?" Audrey eyed Steph who had stopped taking photos and was studying the ground.

Steph swallowed hard. "I've done what I can."

"Good." Audrey jerked her head. "Get up top and get ready to guide the body out."

Steph didn't need to be told twice and scrambled out of the space.

Audrey produced a series of small vials from within her custom suit and proceeded to pluck off maggots of varying sizes into each one. She pulled a small shovel from another pocket and skimmed through the surface dirt around the body, taking additional samples. "The good news is since the body was relatively protected, there's only small animal activity and we don't need to go hunting for missing limbs that a fox or coyote dragged off." She began brushing the maggots off the body and into the dirt away from the path they needed to exit. "Cin, let's clear it off as best we can. Every single one of these little bastards is a biohazard and I don't feel like battling with the administration about it. Corey is that bag set up?"

"Yes." Corey didn't want to talk more than necessary. She was starting to feel light-headed from breathing shallowly or dehydration or both. She'd completely sweated through her scrubs, and it felt like they'd been down there hours but it couldn't have been more than twenty minutes.

"Cin, get on his legs and roll him toward the wall on my count." Audrey placed her hands beneath the shoulders. "Corey, slide the backboard beneath him."

Corey duck walked over the body bag and crouched into position, lining up the backboard.

"One. Two. Three." They rocked the body over and Corey pressed the board hard through the dirt until they could ease the body back down.

"No straps," Audrey instructed. "It will strip the flesh off. On three let's get him in the bag." They gripped the board ends and Corey leaned over to grab the side to guide it in. "One. Two. Three." Audrey gauged the distance to the opening. "Cin, at the head with me. Corey, I need you at the legs to lift him out. Bet you didn't wish you were so strong right about now. You're going to have to do the heavy lifting."

Corey could only nod. She would lift whatever she had to in order to get out of this hole.

The three of them worked together to maneuver the body toward the entrance to the crawlspace, Corey's overtaxed muscles screaming their displeasure the entire way.

"Up," Audrey barked. She and Cin shimmied out, leaving Corey by herself again, alone with her ragged breathing.

Gloved hands reached back in and Corey strained to lift the head end through. They caught their grip and dragged the body out while Corey shuffled quickly to the feet and lifted with effort as they wrestled the body out the gap. Her neck and back muscles burned with the strain, but it was finally through and natural sunlight blinded her as she gazed up.

A gloved and sleeved arm thrust through the opening at her. "Quit fucking around, Curtis," Collier barked.

She reached up and was jerked through the opening.

She blinked at him and he looked her over with what she almost thought was concern.

"All right?"

"Yeah," she gasped, though she didn't feel it. She ripped the face shield off, dragged down her mask and yanked off her hood, breathing deeply.

"Okay." He clapped a hand hard on her shoulder before moving off toward Steph who was stumbling toward the tree line retching, while she struggled out of her gear.

Corey ripped her suit and gloves off, stuffing them into a giant red biohazard bag on the ground and staggered to the back of her truck and the industrial-size tub of cleanser. She pumped handfuls of it and slathered it over her hands, arms, and face, feeling every scrape and paper cut from the last week as the alcohol-based formula touched her skin.

Audrey, a cigarette hanging out the side of her mouth, thrust a bottle of water into her hands. "You did good, kid." She grinned and took a drag so hard her cheeks sunk in.

Corey drained the bottle in seconds, water pouring down her chin before she came up for air. "Got another one of those?" She coughed and wiped her face on the back of her hand.

"You quit." Audrey eyed her but held out her pack of reds.

"Ten years ago." Corey nodded and accepted a light taking a long drag before holding it a beat and exhaling into the sky. "I'd bathe in and guzzle bleach right now if I didn't know I'd die horribly."

Audrey's snort of laughter was the last sound as they smoked and drank another bottle of water each.

Corey looked around the clearing, noticing something was different. "What time is it?"

"Around two. Plenty of time to get the body mechanically defleshed and into boxes. I'm going to get cleaned up and meet you at the morgue with a couple of overeager students in an hour."

Corey blinked stupidly at her. "Where's the ambulance?"

Audrey smiled thinly. "Sergeant Collier knows the plan. He's by the lake. I have to get going and get set up." She squeezed Corey's hand. "Thank you for your help. You have no idea how much I appreciate it."

Corey nodded, unsure what was up. "Anytime."

She grabbed another bottle of lukewarm water and headed around the house to find Collier and Steph passing binoculars back and forth, deep in conversation as they pointed across the lake.

Steph's white T-shirt was soaked through to nearly translucent, her dark bra strap clearly visible. She gave no indication she minded and Collier gave none that he noticed.

"Hey," Corey said wearily. "What now?"

"We need to know who lives there." Collier pointed across the lake to the peaked roof and deck visible through the trees. "We need to go around to the other side and question the owners."

Corey winced. "I can help you with that."

Collier waved her off. "You've done your part."

"I mean…" She sucked in a breath, the air blessedly cleaner on this side. "…I know the owner of that house."

Collier and Steph turned in unison their eyes narrowing, similarly.

Corey pursed her lips. "That's Thayer's place."

Collier blurted. "You're kidding."

"I kid you not."

Steph stared at her hard, her eyes a mixture of sympathy, suspicion, and amusement.

"I need to speak with her," Collier said.

"You know where to find her." Corey dragged her hands through her damp hair and scratched her itchy scalp. "In the meantime, what happened to the ambulance and what are we doing with the body?"

"About that," Collier began. "The ambulance service declined transport in exchange for the backboard."

"So, how is the body getting—" Corey froze as Collier stared at her expectantly, and Steph could no longer meet her eyes. "No. Absolutely not. No fucking way. What happened to the old coroner's van?"

Jackson City was too small to warrant a state run Medical Examiner's office and too far from New York City or Albany to use theirs. Up until a couple of years ago they had been on a county coroner's system. There were three elected coroners—a pediatrician, ENT, and podiatrist—none of whom could actually perform an autopsy. At most they were figureheads in an outdated system that got paid to show up to scenes to say, "Yup, he's dead," and then leave. The county eventually trimmed them entirely out of the budget.

"Got sold at auction last year." Collier shrugged. "You'll get a police escort from Austin and my undying gratitude."

Corey stared daggers at him. "I hate you so much right now." She turned her glare to Steph and jabbed a finger at her. "You too."

The joke was clearly on her when the three of them came back around to the front of the house, which was crawling with police.

The crime scene unit in their own version of protective suits was unloading their van and Cin and Audrey were long gone. Corey watched, dismayed, while two severely underpaid-looking techs loaded the body into the back of her truck. They secured the bag with nylon cord to keep it from sliding around and causing more trauma before slamming the tailgate.

"She can even put the lights on for you," Collier said as they watched the scene unfolding. "I'm going to stay here and supervise this circus."

"Go to hell," Corey growled.

"Don't be like that, Curtis." He gave her shoulder a rough, friendly shake. "You'll get to blow through all the lights and everything."

Corey staggered and bit down on a groan of pain. "Shit."

Collier's expression sobered. "Hey, are you—"

"I'm fine." She gritted out and straightened up. "I need my glasses."

"I got it." He beat her to her truck and retrieved her tinted glasses. "Are you okay to drive? 'Cause Austin can—"

"Fuck that." Corey snatched them out of his hand and flung her cheap ones into the grass. "Fuck those and fuck you."

Corey peered into her truck bed. "Fuck me."

CHAPTER FOUR

Thayer's hand trembled slightly when she reached for the door handle to the doctors' lounge. Damn, her blood sugar was low. It was after two and this was the first time the ED had slowed enough to escape. She was on shift with a first-, second- and third-year resident and Wendy Schilling, a very capable attending in the department. The two women had carried the morning.

There was one other, the fourth-year transfer she mentored as part of her fellowship with the Jackson City Memorial Hospital emergency department. He had been a thorn in her side since the moment he had strutted into the department in a cloud of cologne, despite the fragrance-free policy. His elite upbringing was written in his entitled attitude, veneered tooth grin, and personal trainer physique.

She raided the usually well-stocked refrigerator, pulling out a bottle of water and draining it. She was grateful she was alone when she wiped dribbles from her chin with the sleeve of her white coat. She grabbed a banana and yogurt, wishing she could turn them into a loaded bacon cheeseburger with the power of her mind. She suspected she wouldn't have a hard time convincing Corey to go out to Main Street Burgers later for dinner, or even better, get takeout and cuddle on the sofa with a movie. Something to look forward to.

She dipped the banana in the yogurt while waiting for a fresh pot of coffee. She desperately wanted to get off her feet for a few minutes, but was afraid if she did she'd never get up again. She didn't look up when the door to the lounge banged open and a male voice interrupted her precious minutes of peace. She already knew who it was.

Watson Gregory III, the senator's son, was destined to be an asshole if for no other reason than he had a last name first and first name last. He lived up to it in fine fashion and Thayer winced as his insufferable voice boomed through the room, telling a totally inappropriate story to two impressionable junior residents about a night on daddy's private yacht.

The strangled burble of the coffeemaker signaled its completion and Thayer glanced up to see one cardboard cup on the shelf above her. She reached for it just as his hand pressed into the small of her back and his other hand snatched it away. "Gotta be quicker than that, Reynolds."

She closed her eyes, steeling herself and working to unclench her jaw.

Everyone knew the rumors. He had been bounced from two programs already, and how he'd ended up here was anyone's guess. Though the information was confidential, the why of it was easy to figure out. Watson Gregory III was a bullying, bragging, condescending prick whose air of superiority and self-righteousness was so overt it was almost comical. There was very little that came out of his mouth that wasn't offensive and Thayer had never wanted to punch someone in the throat as badly as she did him.

In fact, she would have asked Corey to show her a few moves if she thought it wouldn't lead to questions—and possibly violence when Corey demonstrated those moves on Watson Gregory herself. Corey would lose her mind if she knew this man walked a floor above her and treated people like he did.

"After you." Thayer smiled icily and moved out of the way while he filled his cup.

She dug a stained drug rep mug out of the sink and washed it.

"That's what I like to see," he said as he sipped his coffee. "A woman who knows her place."

Thayer stilled and she was certain she could hear the junior residents stop breathing. His harassment of her had been far subtler, though never unclear. He addressed her chest when he spoke to her, placed an unnecessary hand against her back and interrupted and talked over her during rounds. The last she usually wasn't bothered by because he was often wrong. His embarrassment on those occasions, instead of tempering his attitude, just seemed to fuel his agenda.

This was the first time he had insulted her so brazenly in front of witnesses and she had but a moment to decide what to do—or what not to do. She finished washing her mug and poured herself a coffee before adding her cream. "Dr. Gregory." She simply nodded to him and the junior residents and left him with his smug smirk still firmly in place.

Thayer flew out the door and nearly slammed into Dana Fowler, her friend since childhood and head nurse of the ED, as she was coming out of the adjacent nurses' lounge. "Shit, sorry, Dana." She cupped a hand around the rim of her mug to keep the coffee from sloshing onto her friend.

"You're in a hurry. You've got some time still if you want to put your feet up."

"It's fine." Thayer shrugged. "I'd rather just power through. There's only a few hours left."

"Excuse me, girls." Watson Gregory came up behind them and made a show of slipping by, a hand brushing against Thayer's back, though there was plenty of room for him to go around them without touching her.

Thayer stiffened and thought about throwing her coffee in his pretentious, carefully stubbled face.

Dana watched him as he headed to the desk before turning back to her friend. "How long are you going to let him get away with that shit, Thayer?"

"What do you mean?"

"Don't give me that. If you think for one second I don't know what's been going on, you're delusional."

She sighed into her coffee mug. "I guess I was hoping if I didn't engage with him he'd get bored and move on."

"To someone else?"

"No, of course not."

"The hospital has a zero tolerance policy for any kind of bullying, harassment, or hostile work environment. All you have to do is say the word and he's out."

She shook her head. "I don't want to—"

"If you say 'cause trouble' I'm going to kick your ass. Because you know as well as anyone this is what got him tossed from the other programs. It's probably daddy's money and influence that's bailed him out and covered his ass so far."

"That's not what I was going to say. And I don't know that and neither do you." The rumor mill ground away at previously unachieved levels with his admission to their program and she wanted nothing to do with it or for Dana to be caught up in it. "Despite the bullshit posturing I think he has the ability to become an excellent physician if he could get over himself and learn something. If I go to Manning or HR it could torpedo his career."

"So, you're protecting him?"

"I'm not protecting him, exactly. I just don't really believe his behavior is for real. It's just so outrageous. It's like he read the idiot's guide on how to be a sexist asshole. If he's as rich as people say he is, why go to medical school at all? It's not like it's easy or glamorous. Why not go into politics? Or why even work? He didn't make it this far on daddy's money. And even if he did, why emergency medicine? Why not plastics or derm?

That's where the money is and you barely have to get your hands dirty. No nights or weekends. The ED is about being on the front lines and helping people."

"If he only knew his best advocate was the woman he's treating like shit." Dana eyed her friend. "What does Corey think about all this? Because I can only imagine—"

"Corey doesn't know about this and she better not hear about it from you."

"Got it." Dana raised her hands in surrender. "But I would like to go on the record for suggesting you tell her and let her rip his throat out."

Thayer smiled grimly. "The thought has crossed my mind. Let's hope it doesn't come to that."

CHAPTER FIVE

Audrey and Cin were waiting for Corey at the loading dock behind the hospital, which served as the rear entrance to the morgue. With them were two other younger graduate students Corey didn't know.

She climbed out of her truck slowly and felt her back and shoulders stiffen. She worked to keep any signs of discomfort from her face lest someone pull rank and send her home.

Audrey grimaced. "I'm really sorry about your truck, Corey. It wasn't my call."

"Yeah, I know." Corey sighed, resigned. Her anger had waned and she just felt drained by the day and disheartened at how much work they still had to do before she could clean out her truck.

Steph came up and touched her shoulder. "I'll help you clean up your truck later," she offered as if reading her mind.

"Thanks." Corey nodded. "I'll get a gurney."

"What do we do now?" Steph stood against the wall with Corey while Audrey directed Cin and the students in the photography and external examination on the body occupying the only stainless steel autopsy table in the room.

"I wait until I'm needed. Is there something else you're supposed to be doing?"

"Just observing and preserving chain of custody for now. If we learn anything I'll pass along the information. When they're ready to move the body over to campus, Kelly Warren is going to take over and I'll probably head back over to the lake and meet up with Collier."

"Warren?" Corey asked. "The kid who found the body, right?"

"He's older than he looks," Steph replied. "I think the sergeant has taken a liking to him. He was first on scene so he's going to keep him involved with the case."

"Well, good for him, I guess."

They were quiet for a few minutes and watched as Audrey set a large black case on the counter and unpacked a handheld object that looked like a cross between a large digital camera and a ray gun. Corey straightened off the wall. "Is that a portable X-ray?"

"It is. I had some leftover grant money last year and finally splurged," she replied. "Anyone who doesn't want to risk radiation-induced cancer or infertility may want to step into the other room."

Corey, Cin, Steph, and the graduate students all crammed into the doorway to the anteroom to watch Audrey scan the body from head to toe, watching the digital display intently and pressing the button to take digital stills as she went.

Steph tapped her foot on the tile floor. "Anything?"

Audrey was running the unit over the torso again. "No. No bullets or embedded knife tips or any other metal to speak of, and no obvious skeletal injury."

Corey asked Steph, "Is that good news or bad?"

"A bullet lodged in his heart would certainly make cause of death easy to determine but I'm not surprised. There wasn't any blood inside or outside the house." She winced, her expression pained.

"Don't worry," Corey offered. "You didn't tell me anything I couldn't figure out on my own. I was down there too. There was no blood. It certainly didn't seem like he was injured and bled out under the house."

Audrey paused her scan over the upper left leg and her brows rose slightly. "Here's something. He has surgical hardware along his left femur—a plate and screws. That should help with identification anyway." She shut the machine down and packed it away. "Corey, you're up if you want to take a look and see if there's anything you can salvage."

Corey raised the mask from around her neck and tapped her face shield down over her glasses. She had changed into dry scrubs, paper gown, and plastic apron—her usual autopsy kit. What was left of the flesh was mottled gray-green and bloated in some places, sunken and sloughing in others. The toes and parts of the feet were shriveled black and desiccated, having been protected in heavy boots. All soft body cavities—eyes, ears, mouth, nose—were mostly eaten away by insects. Corey shuddered and shook off the crawling sensation creeping across her skin.

She shook her head as she snapped on a scalpel blade, knowing there would be nothing useable for her, but they had to go through the motions.

Audrey spoke up as Corey prepared for her Y-incision. "I don't suppose I have to tell you—"

"I'll be careful." Corey nodded and sliced from shoulder to sternum and down, around the navel to the pubic bone releasing a fresh wave of putrid gas into the room. The fans were on full but doing nothing to touch the stench.

"Careful of what?" Steph asked around a cough. The other students continued to observe, take pictures and notes.

"Careful not to hit bone," Cin explained while Corey worked. "It's not something Corey really has to worry about in a routine post because it's the soft tissue and organs we're looking at. In this case that's all useless so we need to analyze the skeleton, and we don't want to introduce any artifact that may be mistaken for real trauma when we get the bones cleaned."

"I get it."

"There's nothing for me to do." Corey's throat burned with bile, her stomach roiling at the site of the rotten innards. She backed away from the table arms raised in surrender and tossed her blade into the Sharps and the handle into the sink. "He's all yours."

"What's next?" Steph asked, swallowing hard when Cin and the graduate students moved back to the body and Corey resumed her place with her against the wall.

"Manually defleshing." She nodded toward the body as all of them got to work scooping out organs and stripping the body of soft tissue as close to the bone without touching it. All the unusable tissue went into a large biohazard bag-lined box for disposal.

"Then what?" Steph's expression held a mix of horror and fascination.

"They'll disarticulate him, put him in a box and drive him to Audrey's lab on campus."

"What about toxicology?"

"On what?" Corey gestured to the table. "He's soup. His eyes are gone so no vitreous. I doubt I could even recognize his bladder. His blood is sludge."

"Hair?"

Corey pursed her lips, considering. She'd never had the occasion to use that and the county lab didn't screen hair. "I don't know. We'd have to send it out to a private lab and someone would have to pay for it."

"If you get me some I'll discuss it with Collier and see if we can put in a requisition."

Cin stood at the head delicately defleshing his face. "Cin, can I have some hair for possible tox screen?"

She nodded without looking up and tugged at the hair. The entire scalp came away with a wet sucking sound and she held it up. "You can have it all."

Corey grimaced. "Just bag it for me. I'll take care of it."

Before she had a chance to do anything else, someone banged hard on the morgue door. She had locked it because she didn't want someone randomly walking in on them. "Be right back."

She pushed the door open to see a female security officer and Dan Lloyd standing behind her. They both took a step back as if being buffeted by strong wind as the door opening changed the pressure in the room and let out a cloud of foul air. Corey quickly stepped into the hall and closed the door. Letting flies out would be a biohazard too. Cleanup would take her hours. Plus, her truck. She groaned inwardly.

Corey's eyes lit up at the security officer. "Kim, when did you get back from mat leave?"

Kim Stewart was taller than Corey at nearly six feet with giant hands that took Jackson City University women's basketball to two Division II championships. She had sharp features, though she wasn't unattractive at all. She was particularly imposing in her uniform, similar to the police but she didn't carry a firearm.

"Last week." Kim gagged and one of the giant hands covered her mouth and nose. "Good lord, Corey, what is going on? We've had complaints about the smell."

Corey peered around her to Dan Lloyd, her physical therapist who worked down the hall from the morgue. He was rocking back and forth on his prosthetic legs, acquired following a motorcycle accident several years ago. He had been instrumental in helping Corey get physically and mentally healthy following her accident. "Complaints from you, Dan?"

"No, not from me. I sure as hell didn't want to come down here and know what you're doing." Dan looked green, his eyes watering. "From my patients. I had to reassure them so I called security." He nodded to her arm. "The arm looks good without the cast. Am I seeing you this week?"

She probably wasn't going to be at the hospital much if she was sticking with the remains on campus. "Actually, something has come up." She hooked a thumb behind her to the door. "And I might be on campus for the rest of the week. Going to have to reschedule for next week, I think."

"Well, don't leave it too long. We gotta get working on that arm, and now that you're on unrestricted duty. I want to make sure you aren't doing anything to set yourself back."

Corey smiled apologetically. "Well, um…"

"Hmm," Dan harrumphed. "That's what I thought. You're the one who's going to pay for it, though, not me."

"Great, can we wrap this up?" Kim interrupted. "Corey, it's really good to see you and I want to catch up. You need to introduce me to your girl, but right now I want to run away and snort bleach up my nose. Can we get this done?"

"You really want to go in there?"

"Hell, no," Kim shot back and edged past her, "but I have to complete the call. I'll be quick. Believe me." The door didn't even have time to close all the way before she came tearing back out. "We're good, thanks."

"I want to see pics of the baby," Corey called after her and Kim waved over her head.

Corey lasted another hour standing and watching the macabre activities as the team sliced through the fibrous ligaments of all the long bones at the joints and carefully packed them in one box. Head, spinal column, flat bones and hands and feet went in another. There was no longer a body— just skeletal remains that would be cleaned of the remaining flesh in Audrey's lab before being expertly reassembled into the complete skeleton and analyzed.

It was close to six when she finally had to sit down, her body aching. It didn't help that she hadn't eaten all day but the idea of food turned her stomach. Steph's promise of help was torpedoed when Collier called to tell her he was keeping Officer Warren with him for a while longer and she needed to go with the remains to the university. Warren would take over later at the lab and another junior officer would observe the overnight. The remains would be processed around the clock until clean and a police officer would be in attendance the entire time.

Everyone had cleared out, cleaning up the larger messes as best they could, but Corey sighed wearily at the smears of gore across the steel table and floor as she lined up bottles of bleach on the counter. And she still had to clean her truck.

CHAPTER SIX

Thayer looked up when she heard Corey's keys in the door and looked at the clock. It was nearly nine. Corey had texted earlier and said she was going to be late and to go ahead and eat but Thayer had never known her to work this late.

She shuffled in and dropped her keys on the counter, kicked off her sneakers with a sigh, and took her glasses off. They had taken to keeping the lights in the condo or Thayer's place dim so she didn't need them at home. "Hey."

"Hi." Thayer closed her laptop. "I was starting to get worried." She rose and crossed the room to slip her arms around Corey's waist, immediately feeling Corey tense and suck in a breath. "Uh-oh." She leaned back and studied her face, the tightness around her mouth and eyes suggesting she was in pain. "What happened?"

She shook her head and gave her a soft kiss on the lips. "Really long day and I may have overdone it a bit." She slipped out of Thayer's grasp and went to the kitchen. "You want a beer?"

"Sure." She didn't really but she knew Corey would bristle if she fussed at her too soon.

She sat back down on the sofa and waited for her, making note of her hunched shoulders and slight left cant as she walked. "Thank you." She accepted the bottle and took a sip while Corey drained half of hers in one go. "You want to tell me about it?"

"Nothing bad. I mean it's bad for someone. Don't even know who yet, but not for me." Corey winced and rolled her shoulders. "Just a hot, labor-intensive gore fest." She made a move to sit next to Thayer on the sofa.

"Hold it." Thayer set her beer on the coffee table before pushing it out of the way, making room for Corey to sit on the floor. "Down here."

"Babe, it's okay. I'm just tired."

"I'll be the judge of that." She appreciated how important Corey's independence was to her, but she made it known when they got back together after she was injured that she would not stand for Corey pretending she was fine or hiding when she was struggling. "Sit."

Corey finished her beer before easing herself down in front of Thayer and stretching her long legs out. Since she'd returned to work, this was a near-nightly ritual: Thayer massaged and stretched Corey's taxed and tense muscles to stave off the spasms and headaches.

"Relax your arms," Thayer instructed and gripped her around each bicep, gently pulling her arms and shoulders backward.

She sucked in a sharp breath, resisting the movement.

"That bad, huh?" Thayer released her arms and moved her hands to her shoulders, pressing her thumbs into the hard muscles where the tension often started.

Corey arched away from her with a groan before settling back down when Thayer eased up on the pressure. "Thanks."

"What's got you all knotted up like this?" Thayer asked, digging her thumbs around her scapula.

"Recovering a decomposed body from inside the crawlspace underneath his house. It was a tight fit."

"Jesus," Thayer breathed, going to work on another stubborn trigger point. "Is that why you smell like bleach?"

"Sexy, huh?" Corey dropped her head when Thayer pressed her thumbs into her neck and worked out the triggers there. "It was either that or smell like rotting, maggot-infested viscera."

"Will you whisper that to me again in bed?" Thayer asked dryly and kissed Corey along the back of her neck.

"Sorry," Corey murmured and let Thayer manipulate her arms again.

"I'm just teasing you, sweetheart." Thayer pulled her arms back again slowly, this time without any painful reaction from Corey. "But I'd prefer to talk about your body when we're in bed."

"Is that what you're limbering me up for?"

She released her arms slowly and ran her hands down her chest, cupping her breasts through her shirt and delighting at Corey's full body shudder. "I will confess getting through my shitty day was fueled by the hope that you might want to take your new arm for a test drive tonight."

Corey leaned back and draped her arms over Thayer's legs, stretching her back and giving Thayer better access to her. "I did. I do."

Thayer slipped her hands down the neck of Corey's shirt and into her bra, circling her nipples and eliciting a gasp from Corey. "I have yet to experience Corey Curtis's two-handed lady loving."

Corey laughed and dropped her head back into her lap, presenting her mouth. "Spiderman kisses."

Thayer closed her mouth over Corey's and plunged her tongue inside. "Mmm." She hummed. "But if you're too sore I can hold out for the morning. I don't have to be in until noon."

Corey reached up and pulled her head down again, capturing her lips upside down. "Come on sunrise."

Thayer sat up abruptly. "Oh, damn it."

"What?" Corey spun around.

"Jim Collier left me a message this afternoon. He wants to meet with me in the morning." She flopped back against the sofa. "I have no idea why. Probably wants some history on a patient or something I can't even talk about—what is that face?"

Corey's lips were pressed tightly together and she looked almost guilty. "I know why he wants to see you."

"Why?"

Corey picked herself up from the floor and joined her on the sofa. "The body we recovered today was at that fishing cabin across the lake from you."

Her brows shot up. "You're kidding." Corey's lips thinned again in response. "You're not kidding."

"I'm sorry." Corey clasped Thayer's hand. "Did you know who lived there?"

"Not really, no. He was older than Nana and I doubt he's still alive. He had some kids though, I think."

"Where are you meeting with Collier?"

"My place at nine."

"I'll come with you."

"You don't have to. You have work."

"I want to," Corey replied. "And I'm actually going to campus. I've been farmed out to help with the skeletal analysis for this case. Dr. Webster wants to be kept in the loop and he's assigned the pathology resident he thinks is getting a fat head to cover autopsy for the rest of the week. Thinks he needs to be taken down a peg or two."

"Oh, god," Thayer groaned. "I have one of those too. Can I send Watson Gregory III to the morgue?" she said in a posh accent.

"In a body bag or out?"

"That's a generous offer. You know I honestly never thought I'd be able to use the label 'dudebro' in a sentence in reference to a professional colleague, but here I am."

"It's timeless and universal, really," Corey joked. "The senator's son, right? The one you were mentoring?"

"Yes." Thayer raked her hands through her hair, which she regretted immediately when she saw Corey's eyes narrow, recognizing it as her stress tell.

"Babe, what's going on?"

"Nothing." She tried valiantly to school her expression into one of calm but knew from the fire igniting in Corey's eyes she was on to her. "I'll handle it," she added, admitting everything with the simple statement.

She'd made every effort not to let Corey know, though it had been troubling her from the beginning and adding totally unnecessary stress to an already intense profession. Thayer knew Corey would react fiercely, and she didn't want to worry her, especially when she was still healing.

"Handle what, exactly?" Corey asked tightly.

"Corey—"

"Tell me, Thayer. If someone is—"

"Corey, I said I will handle it." She cut her off sharply, Corey's eyes widening at her tone. She breathed deeply several times and looked away. "I've been dealing with men like Watson Gregory my entire life, okay? Please, trust me. This is my job, my profession, and I can take care of myself. I have to. Please, tell me you understand."

The muscles in Corey's jaw bunched. "I understand."

Thayer exhaled and placed her hand against Corey's cheek. "I'm okay, sweetheart. I promise. I didn't say anything because I didn't want you to worry about me." She dropped her head and touched her forehead to Corey's. "Are we okay?"

Corey nodded against her. "I trust you, babe. If you say you've got it then that's all I need. But, you know, if you need anything—"

"You will be my first call—always." Thayer tilted her head to kiss her gently. "I love you."

"Ditto." Corey grinned and covered Thayer's mouth with her own.

All other thoughts melted away when she slipped her hands around the back of Corey's neck and pulled her closer, deepening their kiss. "Both hands," she whispered.

A bolt of arousal at her request went straight to Corey's groin, clenching her belly and dampening her briefs as she slid both hands up Thayer's chest, caressing her through her shirt before making short work of the buttons, popping them open all the way down and pulling her blouse open to cup her breasts through her bra.

Thayer moaned and arched her back, her breasts straining against her bra and Corey's hands. "You're sore…"

"Not as sore as you're going to be," Corey growled, expertly flicking the clasp on her bra and freeing Thayer's breasts as she pulled her blouse from her shoulders with one hand and her bra off with the other.

Thayer laughed as Corey pressed her back against the sofa, guiding her down and ravishing her throat with hot, wet kisses while she pulled at Thayer's clothes, flinging each article away as it came free—blouse, skirt, bra, panties.

Corey scrambled out of her jeans and briefs and tore off her shirt and bra, her eyes never leaving Thayer's bright golden gaze as she waited, eyes flashing with arousal.

Corey lowered herself over her, their bodies hot and trembling as they connected fully, Thayer stretched out beneath her. "It's like my first time." Corey grinned lasciviously as she ran both her hands up and down Thayer's body. "How do you like me now?"

Thayer writhed beneath her, igniting Corey's desire to monumental levels. She stilled her lover by sinking her weight against her, spreading her legs with a thigh between them as

Thayer laced her hands through her short hair and pulled her down to cover her mouth.

Corey broke away covering one breast with one hand, the other with her mouth and slid her right hand down between Thayer's legs, tickling a path through her soaked curls and parting her center.

Thayer bucked her hips as Corey teasingly stroked her most sensitive skin with her fingertips.

"Now, Corey, please," Thayer gasped, arching against her touch.

Corey didn't make her wait any longer. She wanted it just as badly and slid two fingers inside her to the sound of Thayer's satisfied sigh as she was filled with her hand, her thumb circling her clit slowly.

"Oh." Thayer's lips parted, her eyes closing to slits while Corey stroked slowly in and out of her. "That's perfect." She clutched at Corey's shoulders pulling and pushing in rhythm with her hips. "Yes."

Corey added a third finger and pressed her knee against her own hand as she went deeper, adding to the pressure. Thayer jolted at the sensation with a cry of surprise and gasped, her eyes rolling. "Oh, god, that's it."

Corey increased her pace and pressure, rocking against Thayer's thrusts and driving deep into her with her weight while threading her left hand through her hair to hold her head back against the sofa and arch her neck so Corey could attack it with her mouth. "I don't have enough hands," Corey groaned, raking her teeth down Thayer's throat.

"Plenty," Thayer gasped, clutching across Corey's back, nails digging into her skin as her thrusts grew frantic and her chest heaved to draw breath. "You have...oh, shit..."

Corey worked to keep up with her when Thayer rocked and bucked against her as her climax roared through her in waves for several long seconds before she collapsed back against the sofa with a satisfied sigh.

"Damn, woman." Corey grinned at her glassy look. "I kind of hoped that would take longer."

"I'm not sorry." She rolled her eyes to the floor and the piles of clothes. "Though, I do wish you'd be gentler on my clothes."

She followed her gaze. "But it's like unwrapping the best present on Christmas morning every time." She peppered soft kisses across Thayer's chest.

Thayer threaded her fingers through Corey's hair. "Well, maybe you could try being the kid who doesn't want to tear the paper. It's getting expensive."

"Not a chance." She circled her tongue around a nipple.

Thayer squirmed and pushed her away, gently. "Stop. I'm not ready."

Corey relented and rolled over onto her elbow to prop herself up. "You could always just be naked around the house. That would work for me."

She scowled playfully. "Give my bank account a thought next time, please."

"We've been over this." She grinned. "Your bank account is all I think about."

"Where did you get the idea that I have money? Do you have any idea how much I owe in school loans? But I suppose I'll allow it since I only want you for your hard body."

"That's what I like to hear." Corey laughed and kissed her gently for a long time. "Can I take you to bed?" She sat up and pulled Thayer up with her.

"Don't you want something to eat?" Thayer asked.

Corey grinned wickedly. "I was just going to ask you the same thing."

CHAPTER SEVEN

Corey was in the crawlspace again. It was impossibly hot and dark and her body was heavy and sluggish. She tried to stand but banged the back of her head on the underside of the house. Over and over again she tried to get out, her head pounding.

Her eyes shot open with a sharp gasp. She was in her room and it was full dark. She could tell by the stillness of the night that it was nowhere near dawn. She was hot with Thayer's naked body draped partially across her, heavy in sleep.

The unpleasant dream was just that but the pounding in her head was very real. The dull throbbing ache at the base of her skull signaled the beginning of a migraine, payment for surviving a fall that could have just as easily killed her.

"Shit." She breathed and tried to raise her free arm to the back of her neck but was stopped when a streaking hot pain shot through her right shoulder, a gift from her excessive physical exertion of the day.

She glanced at the clock as she extricated herself from under Thayer, hearing her stir. It was just past one in the morning and she took comfort that she still had time to head off the migraine or sleep it off before morning.

"What's wrong?" Thayer asked in a gravelly voice.

"Nothing. Go back to sleep," Corey murmured as she stumbled to the bathroom. She squinted against the harsh light while she fumbled through the cabinet and her medication bottles. She just wanted a muscle relaxant but couldn't read the labels.

Thayer spoke softly from behind her. "How bad is it?"

"It's still early. I just need something." Corey massaged the back of her neck and tried to reach the epicenter of her tension around her right shoulder blade.

"Can you hold off for a few minutes? I have something for you to try." Thayer offered her hand and led her back to bed leaving the bathroom light on to cast a glow into the room.

She dropped back into bed with a groan and huddled on her side as she listened to Thayer move around the room before feeling her weight on the bed.

"Lie on your stomach, sweetheart." Thayer encouraged her to stretch out on her front with her arms up around her head. "Is that okay?"

"Yeah." She heard the snap of a cap and Thayer rubbing her hands together before they came down gently on her back, slick and warm with oil and the smell of peppermint and coconut filled the room. "Mmm," Corey groaned as Thayer eased her oiled hands around her shoulders and neck, massaging her spasming muscles.

"Tell me where."

"My right shoulder. Underneath the scapula. Something really hurts."

Thayer slid her hands over and dug her thumbs into the muscles, hitting the large knot immediately. "I got it."

"Yeah."

"Just breathe," Thayer whispered and worked at the trigger, relaxing the bunched muscle fibers and smoothing the knot. "You know, in retrospect, perhaps we should have skipped the nighttime extracurriculars considering your strenuous day."

"Mmm," Corey mumbled. "That's not the part of my day I wish had gone differently."

"Well, perhaps exercise more caution next time."

"Caution's for suckers."

"You should really rethink your personal motto."

"Maybe."

"What do think of this oil?" Thayer spoke softly as she continued easing the tension in her back and pressed her thumbs into the base of Corey's head.

"'s nice," Corey slurred, her eyes growing heavy.

"Peppermint oil is a natural muscle relaxant and I've had patients who swear by it." Thayer ran her hands over her one more time. She wiped her hands on a towel and pulled the sheet over them both as she lay down next to Corey, their heads close together.

"Thank you for loving me so well." Corey sighed happily.

"You make it very easy."

Corey slept hard the rest of the night and woke refreshed, if still a little sore. She could hear the shower running and checked the time. It was just past seven and Thayer needed to head out to her place to meet Collier and Steph about her neighbor.

She ran through a series of stretches on her bedroom floor to loosen and warm up her muscles, though she didn't expect to be doing anything more strenuous than standing around today and likely tomorrow as well. She could safely save herself for their nighttime activities.

"Good morning." Thayer came out of the bathroom on a cloud of steam, running a comb through her thick auburn curls. "Feeling better?"

"Yeah." Corey picked herself up off the floor. "You're up early. I thought you said nine."

"I did." Thayer rummaged through Corey's drawers pulling out her own bra and panties a pair of her own jeans and one of Corey's T-shirts. "I've been here so often lately that I have nothing at home to offer them, so I want to run to the store." Thayer threw her wet hair up into a hasty knot at the top of her head.

Corey snorted. "Babe, they're not your guests. They're coming to question you."

Thayer's head snapped up, her eyes wide. "Question me?"

"Not question. I'm sorry." She shook her head. "Interview."

"Whatever." Thayer scowled. "I can still offer them some coffee."

"Well, hang on a few minutes and we'll swing by Rachel's coffee shop and get her to hook us up. We have time." Corey headed for the bathroom satisfied with her suggestion. She hadn't seen her best friend in a few days and they were due for some catching up.

"I'm pretty sure Rachel's not going to be able to take a break to serve us first thing on a weekday morning. I don't want her to get in any trouble."

Corey barked a laugh from the shower. "In trouble? She owns the place."

"I beg your pardon? Rachel owns the Old Bridge Coffee House?"

"Uh..." Corey poked her soapy head out the shower door and winced. "Shit."

"Am I not supposed to know? Why not?"

"I'm sorry, babe," Corey called from the shower. "It's not you. Hardly anyone knows. Rachel likes it like that. She didn't want to ruin her slacker reputation by people finding out she's a competent and successful business owner."

"Wow, that's incredible and I totally believe that about her." Thayer laughed. "Her secret is safe with me. I won't tell anyone or let on I know."

"No, that's silly." She stepped out and quickly toweled off. "You should know. We'll swing by and talk to her."

"Who's driving? Are we taking two cars?" Thayer called from the stairs as she headed down.

"Um, no." Corey pulled on clothes and finger combed her short hair. "You're driving. I left my truck at the hospital last night. I really didn't feel like getting back in it." She took the stairs two at a time and nearly slammed into Thayer at the bottom looking very unhappy.

"How did you get home?" Thayer challenged.

She shrugged and moved to step around her. "I walked."

Thayer moved with her, blocking her, her brow arched, disapprovingly.

Corey raised her hands in surrender. "Next time I'll call you."

CHAPTER EIGHT

"Holy, Mary…" Corey whistled at the jammed downtown street in front of The Old Bridge Coffee House. The shop took up the first floor of a city original, a three-story brick building owned by the law firm, Tagliotti, Mancini and Castiglione. The firm used the top two floors and a side entrance from the parking lot. Corey always thought with a name like that they should be involved with organized crime. Every time she joked about it in the shop, Rachel glared her to silence which only fueled her speculation. The Old Bridge customers parked on the street and today cars packed end to end against the curb and there was a line of people out the door. "What the hell is going on?"

"Hold on." A car pulled out on the opposite side of the street and Thayer gunned her Range Rover around and whipped into the spot.

"Pretty slick, Slick." Corey grinned.

"What's that one from?" Thayer asked as she opened the door.

"*The Abyss.*" Corey beamed, pleased that Thayer even recognized it as a quote. "One day I'm going to see if I can communicate entirely in movie quotes."

"Not with me you won't. I don't even know how you keep all these lines in your head."

"I am a font of useless and whimsical pop culture and film knowledge." Corey reached for Thayer's hand and they jogged across the street.

They threaded their way through the small groups of young people milling around the sidewalk in front of the large glass window that made up the front, drinking coffee and tea and snacking on every manner of pastry. The lower inside of the glass was papered with twice as many colorful advertisements as last time Corey had been there. She couldn't actually remember when that was.

The inside was buzzing with activity. The line at the counter wrapped around the inside of the shop, every table was full and people were packed elbow to elbow at the high bar at the front window.

Corey craned to see over the line behind the counter. There were at least six baristas working, foaming coffee, warming muffins, steeping tea, and ringing people out. The lights were bright and Corey was dizzy with the visual and auditory assault. "Je-sus," she muttered and adjusted her glasses.

"Are you all right?" Thayer asked, her mouth close to Corey's ear.

"Yeah, it's just—"

"Hey, Corey."

Corey's head whipped back and forth at her name, finally looking up to the ladder that rolled back and forth behind the counter so staff could reach items from the floor-to-ceiling shelves that lined the back red brick wall.

"Jude?" Corey's mouth gaped at the goofily grinning guy halfway up the wall. She watched as he dropped a five-pound burlap sack of beans to another man at the bottom. Jude was Jude Weatherly of Weatherly's Funeral Home. She had only ever seen him picking up bodies from her at the morgue and had, around the time she started seeing Thayer, half-jokingly set him up with Rachel.

"Rachel's at the back," he yelled over the din. "You want coffee?"

Corey nodded dumbly and gripped Thayer's hand, leading her toward the back of the long shop.

"Who was that?" Thayer asked.

"Tell you in a minute." Corey raised her voice as they passed beneath a speaker. She couldn't help but notice she really liked the singer—a husky-voiced woman playing amazing guitar.

Rachel was at a round table all the way at the back. She had a laptop open and stacks of paper splayed out in front of her. She was dressed in her usual cargo shorts, battered chucks, and black coffeehouse T-shirt, which showed off lean muscles and a wide array of tattoos over both arms. She had gotten a haircut and her always-spiky black hair was now in a faux hawk. She was just standing and shaking the hand of a young woman looking barely out of her teens who smiled and disappeared into the crowd.

"Hey, gorgeous." Rachel beamed at Thayer and came around from behind the table to hug her. "To what do I owe this absolute pleasure?"

She returned the embrace. "I'll let Corey tell you."

"Are we interrupting something?" Corey held the chair for Thayer and grabbed another one to swing around for herself.

"Just another day at the office." Rachel gestured to her bustling shop and closed her laptop as she sat back down. "I'm interviewing for a few positions today, but I don't have another one for a half hour so I'm all yours."

"Here you go, ladies." Jude appeared out of the crowd with a tray of three steaming coffee mugs, creamers, and sweeteners.

"Aw, thanks, dude." Rachel smiled at him affectionately as he bused up the two empty mugs littering her table.

"Welcome, dude." He returned her gaze briefly and then turned to Thayer and held out his hand. "You must be Thayer.

I've heard a lot about you. I'm Jude, a friend slash coworker of Corey's and a friend slash employee of Rachel's."

Thayer shook his hand, returning his smile. "Very nice to meet you, Jude."

"Um, Jude, you work here now?" Corey asked, her eyes flicking between him and Rachel.

"Yeah, sometimes, I guess." He shrugged. "I like it."

"What about your dad and the funeral home?" Corey asked.

"Oh, business is booming as always and I'm still the heir. You know, though, most of the days there I deal with my customers in the absolute shittiest moments of their lives, so spending time here really makes me feel…"

"Alive?" Rachel suggested.

"Yeah, I guess that's it." Jude nodded. "I better run. I'm sure I'll see you soon, Corey. Nice to meet you, Thayer."

Corey turned to Rachel. "Are you two dating?"

Rachel's mouth quirked into a smile. "We're having fun when the mood strikes us. No expectations and that seems to suit us both at the moment."

"He's cute," Thayer commented as she sipped her coffee.

"He is that," Rachel agreed. "Now, what brings you to my humble establishment?"

Corey exhaled a breath. "Well, I was going to confess that I slipped up this morning and revealed your true nature to Thayer but you don't seem too concerned about anyone knowing, so what gives?"

Rachel's eyes widened as she sipped her coffee. "First, I can't believe you hadn't already told her."

"Well, you're not exactly pillow talk," Corey snarked and Thayer coughed on her coffee. "And I promised you I wouldn't tell anyone."

"And second, that ship has sailed, my friend." Rachel searched her table, lifting papers until she found a thick glossy magazine and tossed it across to them. It was the Best of the City issue of *JC Magazine*.

"Hey, that's you." Rachel was grinning broadly on the cover in front of her business. Thayer thumbed it open and started skimming the article.

Corey cocked her head to look at the cover while Thayer read. "Holy shit, man, you're on the cover."

"I know, right?" Rachel beamed. "I came in first in two of the categories, Best Coffee Shop and Best Local Color."

Corey's brow furrowed. "How did I not know any of this?"

Rachel's eyes flicked to Thayer who was reading intently. "You've been a little busy."

"Still, though." Corey leaned over to offer her fist, which Rachel bumped. "I'm proud of you."

"Thanks," Rachel said. "So you didn't brave the hipster throngs to congratulate me. Is that what you came to say? That you—what—violated my confidence?"

"Well, yeah," Corey admitted.

Rachel barked a laugh. "Jesus, Cor, you really are a boy scout."

Thayer smiled and nodded, letting them know she was also paying attention to more than the article.

Corey flushed with embarrassment and hid behind her mug. "I prefer girl scout," she muttered. "And there was something else."

"Hit me," Rachel said as Thayer set the magazine aside.

"Collier and his partner are meeting us at Thayer's place this morning to speak with her and we haven't been there in a few days and are a little short on rations."

"Say no more, my wayward friends." Rachel pushed herself up from the table. "One of my new enterprises is catering and we had this big order from JC Bank and Trust this morning and the meeting got canceled at the last minute." Rachel motioned them to follow. "It's already paid for but I can't really put it back in the display shelf so it's all yours."

Corey's eyes widened at how the crowds parted as Rachel walked through the shop and she and Thayer shared an amused glance.

"Jude, grab that tray for the bank will you?" Rachel called across the counter.

He slid an enormous plastic-covered tray laden with pastries and fruit over to her.

"And the coffee box, please, and the bag of condiments," Rachel added.

Rachel heaved the stack of containers into Corey's arms. "To Collier, with my love. And don't think you're going to get away with not telling me what this is about later. And since when does Collier have a partner?"

"Yeah, yeah," Corey agreed and adjusted the weight. "Tell you another time."

Thayer took the coffee box off the top before Corey dropped it all. "That's very generous, Rachel, thank you."

"Oh, I almost forgot." Rachel leaned across the counter and grabbed a stack of hot pink squares of paper. "I got my beer and wine license, too, and one Friday a month is going to be local talent events. Singer-songwriter kind of stuff. This Friday is Cam Delmar. She's playing right now." She gestured to the speakers in the ceiling. "These are VIP passes. I was going to hand them out tonight at the gym but you're here now so take them and come if you can." She reached around and tucked the paper into Corey's back pocket. "Make sure Jules and Dana get one too, otherwise it's a twenty-dollar cover."

Thayer's face lit up. "Oh, fun. Friday night starts my once in a blue moon weekend off. We'll be here."

Corey grunted and shifted the tray in her arms. "What she said."

"Get out of here." Rachel waved them off. "You're holding up the line."

CHAPTER NINE

Corey set the tray on the dining table and pulled the insulated box of coffee off the top.

"How much time do I have?" Thayer called from the kitchen.

She checked her watch. "Twenty minutes or so."

"Good." She came around and set four mugs on the table before brushing her lips over Corey's. "I'm going to change and do something with my hair."

Corey slipped her arms around her waist and pulled her closer. "You have lots of time before your shift. What's wrong with what you're wearing?" She kissed Thayer again, deeply.

Thayer wriggled out of her arms and headed down the hall. "Because the police are coming to interview me and I would like to look presentable."

"Hey," Corey called after her. "You're wearing my shirt. What are you saying?"

"Nothing at all, sweetheart," she sang sweetly from the bedroom. "I love you basic."

"Basic?"

"You're low maintenance and easy to shop for and if we both took as long as I do to get ready, we'd never go anywhere."

"That's a fair point."

When the front door banged fifteen minutes early, she opened it to see Collier in his chronically ill-fitting suit and Steph Austin in her crisp uniform, both in matching aviators.

"Curtis," Collier greeted. "Why am I not surprised to see you?"

Corey leaned against the door and fought a smile. "Because you know I'm having hot girl on girl sex with your person of interest?"

She delighted in the color that rushed to his face and Steph pressed her lips together looking like she wanted to laugh.

"First of all, she's not a person of interest. She's a potential witness so don't get your knickers in a twist. Second of all, there's no need to brag. Can we come in?"

She stepped back and motioned grandly for them to enter. They both removed their glasses like it had been choreographed.

"This place is gorgeous," Steph said, walking to the back sliders to look out at the lake.

"Thayer is getting ready for work. She'll be out in a minute. In the meantime…" She gestured to the spread on the table. "We have snacks, so help yourself."

Collier grunted and poured himself a mug of coffee and palmed two pastries cramming one right into his mouth.

"With love from Rachel Wiley, by the way," Corey added with a wink.

Collier eyed her and chomped down on his food dramatically.

Corey turned at the sound of Thayer's heels on the hardwood as she emerged from the hall and stopped breathing, as she often did, when she saw her dressed to impress. She was wearing the black skirt that hugged her hips and flared around her legs to mid-calf and a gold blouse that matched her eyes.

Her hair was dry and auburn curls fell past her shoulders held back from her face with a gold clip.

"Jim, good morning. It's good to see you." She extended her hand and Corey grinned at how hard he swallowed as he took it. "I hope I didn't keep you waiting."

"Hey, Doc, been a while." He nodded toward Steph who was looking at Thayer in a way that made Corey wonder if she was correct about her being straight. "My, um, associate, Officer Steph Austin."

Thayer offered her hand. "Pleased to meet you, Officer Austin."

"You as well, Dr. Reynolds."

"Call me Thayer." She poured herself a cup of coffee and headed to the living room. "We can be informal, right?"

Corey knew Thayer's excessive charm was masking her nervousness and followed her closely.

She glanced back to see Collier snatch another pastry but Steph met her eyes, flicked her glance to Thayer and arched an appreciative brow her direction.

Corey couldn't help her proud smirk as she settled on the sofa next to Thayer.

Steph and Collier took the opposite sofa and Collier brushed crumbs off his lap as he sat forward, setting his mug on the coffee table between them. "Sorry to disrupt your morning, but I'm sure Curtis has told you about the scene yesterday."

Thayer crossed her legs and glanced at Corey with a small smile. "In more detail than was necessary, yes."

Collier reached into his pocket and produced his notebook, flipping it open. "Do you know who lives on that property?"

"I'm not certain. If memory serves, the original owner was Albert Crandall. I never knew him and I don't think he was still using the place when I started spending my summers here. He may have had some children. I don't really recall and my grandmother didn't discuss other lake residents with me. Most folks live out here for the peace and tranquility, not block parties. He was quite old, though. I would be shocked if he were still alive."

"He's not," Collier replied. "Died at eighty-five from lung cancer. Survived by two sons, Edward and Harold, and one grandson, Robert, by his eldest son, Edward. Edward inherited the property ten years ago and the title is still in his name. He died three years ago in a car accident. We're having a hard time tracing who uses the property now."

"I'm sorry, I have no idea. I would assume the other brother, right? I've only been back a couple of months and I work a lot, and, otherwise..." Her gaze flicked to Corey. "I've been busy."

"Hmm." Collier jotted notes.

Steph asked, "Dr. Reynolds, um, Thayer, have you noticed any unusual road traffic in the area recently?"

"Unusual? I'm not even sure what usual traffic looks like. I'm here and gone at odd hours and sometimes..." she glanced at Corey again, "...not home for days. There is traffic. Old South meets up with the highway in about twenty more miles. There are tractor-trailers. There are boaters, of course, and a launch down the road from here. It's a pretty drive along the lake so I would expect to see leaf peepers in the fall."

"The house across the lake. Do they have a boat?" Steph asked.

"Sure. Everyone on the lake does, I think." Thayer sat back against the sofa. "Quite a nice black fishing boat with glitter finish."

Both Collier's and Steph's eyes narrowed at Thayer. "You're that familiar with it?" Collier asked.

Corey felt Thayer tense and moved imperceptibly closer to her.

"I see it, yes," Thayer replied, glancing between them. "I enjoy watching the lake traffic when I can."

"Who owns it?"

"I have no idea. I've only ever seen men on it, though, if it comes close enough."

"How often do you see it?"

"I don't know." She shrugged, helplessly. "A couple of times a month maybe."

"Doing what?"

"Boating."

Corey could feel Thayer's tension, and her own was ratcheting up a notch. Her anger was simmering at the way Collier was firing questions at her like he was attempting to catch a suspect in a lie. Thayer could take care of herself, though, so Corey reined herself in and remained quiet.

Collier went on. "What about Lillian Thayer?"

"What about her?" Thayer stiffened, visibly, at the mention of her grandmother whose house they were living in while Lillian had moved to a very nice assisted living residence following a stroke a few years ago. Corey clenched her jaw in response to their abruptness.

"Would she know the owners?"

"You would have to ask her."

Collier checked his notes. "You're her power of attorney and medical proxy."

"I am, for when the time comes that she cannot make competent and informed decisions on her own behalf. But I assure you, now is not that time."

"We'll speak with her, then."

"I would encourage you to be honest about what it is you want to know upfront as she may not be nearly as patient and forgiving as I am," she said coolly.

Corey nearly stood up and cheered when Collier's face reddened in embarrassment and Steph looked equally chagrined.

He closed his book and tucked it into his pocket. "Look, Doc, we didn't come here to bust your, um, chops."

Corey couldn't hold back any longer and drilled him with a glare. "Then why don't you talk to us like human beings and tell us what you want to know?"

He glowered at her. "Stay out if it, Curtis."

"Stay out of it?" Corey stood before she knew what she was doing. "I'm already in it. Elbow deep in a rotting corpse. I didn't see you under that house."

He got to his feet and jabbed a finger in her direction. "Do I tell you how to do your job?"

"All the goddamn time." She took a step toward him and felt Thayer's hand on her arm.

"Corey, it's okay." She pulled her back a step.

Steph was on her feet, looking anxiously between Collier and Corey as she smoothly stepped between them while they glared at each other.

"Boy," Thayer commented lightly into the charged silence, "that escalated quickly."

Corey blinked, her anger diffusing. She turned to Thayer. "That was really funny, babe."

"Like that?" Thayer flashed her dazzling smile, her eyes shining.

Like a fog lifting, the tension dissipated and the room seemed brighter.

Collier grumbled, "I'm going to get more coffee."

"Thayer, Corey, please sit," Steph said. "Let's start over and we'll tell you what we're thinking."

CHAPTER TEN

As if carrying the proverbial olive branch, Collier returned with the box of coffee and topped up everyone's mug before he took his place back on the sofa next to Steph who watched him expectantly.

"Go ahead," he offered and sipped his coffee. "I'm obviously way out of my league here."

Corey snorted a laugh and rolled her eyes at his wounded male ego. Now that it seemed they were back on friendly territory, she moved over next to Thayer and rested a hand casually on her leg. Thayer placed her hand over Corey's and gave her fingers a squeeze.

"So, from the beginning." Steph took a breath. "Three years ago the department purchased a program called Critical Stats. It's a pretty simple algorithm that runs in the background nonstop and reviews crime stats for the city. The parameters are set at whatever level is decided is normal or acceptable. If arrest rates, crimes reported, civilian complaints, and a whole host of other metrics deviate from what's expected from past years, either significantly or for a sustained period of time, an alert goes out to a couple analysts. If it's a real trend and the brass decide it's worth looking at, we drill down to see what's going on."

"Okay." Corey nodded. "So you've learned something?"

"Yes," Steph replied. "We received an alert that drug-related crime is up nine percent and rising over the last six months."

"That's certainly significant," Thayer mused.

"So far it's mostly been nonviolent crime—vandalism, possession, small quantity distribution, theft, break-ins, and the like."

"So far, meaning you expect the nature of the crimes to evolve?" Thayer asked.

"Inevitably and not in the good *mature* and *progress* way." Steph smiled grimly.

"What kind of drugs are we talking about?" Corey asked.

"Meth."

Thayer's brows rose. "Methamphetamine? That seems unusual."

"You mean someone's gone all *Breaking Bad* in JC?" Corey asked incredulously.

"We don't think it's being cooked here," Steph explained. "You must see your share of drug users come through the hospital."

"Sure," Thayer agreed, "but I would argue I see more opioid abusers these days—Oxy and fentanyl. Heroine, of course."

"Any change recently?" Steph sat forward. "For either of you?"

Thayer and Corey exchanged a glance. "Not that I've noticed," Thayer replied. "But, again, I haven't been here long. The hospital has a bio stats department that runs similar programs looking for trends. You might check with them."

"We'll do that," Steph agreed. "Corey?"

Corey shrugged. "I see them but I can't say I've noticed an increase in ODs. I was also out of work for nearly a month."

"It just may be too soon to see the more severe side effects of a drug epidemic here," Steph explained. "Which is why we need to get a handle on it before we do."

"Handle on what?" Corey asked.

Steph's gaze flicked to Collier and he inclined his head slightly. "We think someone new is bringing the drugs in from the city and starting up a distribution network here and moving them upstate and south into Pennsylvania."

"A drug ring?" Thayer asked. "Here?"

"Yes," Steph agreed.

"And you think this has something to do with the body we found?" Corey asked.

"There was evidence at the scene to suggest someone who used that house was a frequent drug user." Steph seemed to hesitate. "And, we do have a working theory."

"Which is?" Corey prodded.

Collier sat forward to join the conversation, his confidence apparently recovered. "In many of our recent arrests the perps have some connection to the lake and fishing."

"Fishing," Thayer repeated.

Corey's gaze darted between Steph and Collier, their expressions matching in seriousness. "Is that like the bank robbers are surfers? The drug dealers are anglers?"

Collier stared at her. "I have no idea what that means but points for using 'anglers' in a sentence."

"Saw it on a bumper sticker," she quipped.

"What connection?" Thayer asked.

"We can't really go into that with you." Steph smiled apologetically.

"Should we be concerned?" Thayer asked. "I mean about staying here."

Steph shook her head. "I think it's way too soon to get that excited about it. Like I said it's only a theory, but we are pursuing it. First we need to identify the body and get a timeline and possible cause of death before we can draw any conclusions." She paused to consider a moment. "But if you don't feel safe here, by all means, stay in town." Her eyes moved to Corey. "I'm sure you can find a place."

"On the other hand," Collier added, "if you wanted to take a turn spending some time out here and enjoy watching boat traffic, you're welcome to keep us apprised of anything interesting going on. That would help too."

"Doing your grunt work?" Corey asked.

He shrugged. "Don't have enough yet to warrant any overtime for surveillance. I'll take what I can get."

Steph stood. "We really appreciate your time, Thayer, and I apologize for before. We shouldn't have been so badgering. If you would like to get in touch with your grandmother and let her know we'll be contacting her, that might help smooth the way for us."

"I will, thank you." Thayer smiled and offered her hand. "It was nice to meet you, Officer Austin."

"Steph, please." She shook her hand. "And if there's anything else you can think of, please call either myself or Sergeant Collier."

"Of course." Thayer nodded.

Collier cleared his throat and eyed Corey as he rose from the sofa. "Are we cool, Curtis?"

"Well, I am." Corey grinned crookedly. "You're a bit uptight."

"You're hilarious." He turned to Thayer. "Before we go, Doc, you mind if we take a look from your deck?"

"Please." Thayer gestured to the door. "There are binoculars on the table by the slider."

"Thanks." Collier and Steph moved off.

Corey turned to Thayer. "Well, that was fun."

Thayer slipped her hands around Corey's waist and rested her head against her chest. "Not my favorite way to start the day. I really thought you were going to hit him."

She wrapped her arms around Thayer's shoulders. "I really wanted to. Man, that guy can piss me off."

Thayer breathed a laugh. "That's because you two are cut from the same cloth."

"That's crap."

Thayer looked at her. "In no particular order I would describe Jim Collier as stubborn, honorable, passionate, sensitive, and fiercely protective of those he cares about. Sound like anyone you know?"

Corey arched a brow. "What about sexy, sensual, and alluring?"

Thayer smiled and kissed her softly. "I'm sure he's those things to someone but not to me."

Corey deepened their kiss and threaded her hands through her hair. She came up for air and asked, "Know anyone who is?"

"Mmm." Thayer purred, pressing herself into another kiss for a moment before pulling away. "Enough. I need to finish getting ready for work and call Nana. Are you waiting and riding in with me?"

Corey let her go. "I think I'll grab a ride in with the Five-O. I need to get over to campus. Can I come by later and see if you have time for a quick bite?"

"Yes, please," Thayer replied. "I can't make any promises though."

CHAPTER ELEVEN

Corey drove toward the Emergency Department entrance, Steph riding shotgun with the tray of pastries and coffee on her lap. She was going to drop them off in the ED before they headed to Audrey's lab. "You notice Collier barely slowed down at my truck to let us out?"

"How could I not? I almost had to tuck and roll," Steph replied. "I think he's still smarting from earlier."

"Yeah, sorry about that. I hope I haven't caused problems between you."

"We went about that conversation all wrong," Steph admitted. "You and Thayer were right to call us out, although I could have done without the impending violence."

"Yeah, I know I can be a bit of a hothead, and I don't know what it is, but I lose my cool with him faster than just about anyone."

"That's because you two are so much alike."

"Oh, god. Not you too," Corey groaned. "Thayer just said the same thing to me."

"She's a smart woman." Steph paused. "And, I have to say, positively stunning."

Cory grinned. "You noticed."

"Does anyone not?"

"Nope."

Steph turned to look at her. "And how does that work out for you?"

She shrugged. "As long as she's okay with it, I am too."

"Are you really?"

"Well, I kind of have to be."

"Mmm. Thayer doesn't really strike me as the kind of woman who would suffer the jealous girlfriend well. And if she's not okay with it? What then?"

Corey arched a brow at her. "Then the gloves come off."

"Has that happened?" Steph asked.

Corey pulled into a fifteen-minute pickup and drop-off spot outside the ED main entrance. "Not yet."

She took the tray and coffee from Steph's lap and balanced the still mostly full box of coffee on top. "I'll just be a few minutes."

"I'll come in with you." Steph hopped from the truck. "Can I carry something?"

"Nah, I got it." Corey glanced back at her as she headed toward the entrance. "Your job is to protect me if I get mobbed by starving nurses and residents."

"Corey, get back." Steph grabbed her arm and hauled her backward several steps as a black Hummer H2 roared into the accessible parking spot right where she was about to cross.

Corey staggered, the box of coffee sliding off its perch and exploding on the ground at their feet, showering them both from the knees down. "What the fuck, man?" Corey shouted at the driver.

A tall, perfectly groomed and coiffed man jumped down, whipped on his white coat and shot Corey and Steph a satisfied smirk over his shoulder. "Watch where you're walking, Glasses."

Corey seethed, her teeth grinding together. "Oh, that's gotta be him."

"Who?" Steph picked up the coffee box and held it up carefully to stop the spill as she eyed the obnoxious SUV.

"The 'not yet' from your question about Thayer."

"Do you know him?" Her brow furrowed as she studied the rear of the truck.

"Not formally, no." Corey took a deep breath. "He's Watson Gregory III, a fourth-year resident Thayer was mentoring as part of her fellowship and his orientation."

Her eyes widened. "Any relation to the senator?"

"Yup." She pushed through the main doors and headed to the nurses' station.

"Corey." Jules Archer, a young nurse and friend of Corey and Thayer's, practically squealed. "And you have treats? Those are for us, right? I'll just go stash this in the lounge." She snatched the tray from Corey's hands and skipped away.

"Maybe today won't suck after all," Dana said as Jules disappeared. "Hey, why aren't you at work, anyway? And why the police escort?"

"Oh, right." Corey turned to Steph. "Steph Austin this is Dana Fowler, Thayer's BFF."

Dana extended her hand over the counter and greeted Steph. "Nice to meet you."

"You too. Corey and I are going to the same place. She's consulting on a case for us."

Dana glanced at Corey. "Do tell."

"Another time. I promise." Corey eyed the Hummer she could see through the glass doors. "Hey, does that Gregory dude always park like an asshole?"

Dana followed her gaze, her face darkening. "He does everything like an asshole if he thinks he can get away with it."

"We'll fucking see about that," Corey muttered and reached for the phone over the counter, jamming in a number and waiting for the line to connect. "Good morning. Is Kim Stewart on today? Great. Can you radio her and let her know Corey Curtis needs her in the ED? Yes, now. Thank you." She hung up and turned to the other women, her mouth twisting into a wicked grin.

A few minutes later Kim strode in, her security uniform crisp and polished, and her long legs carrying her across the floor in half the time of an average-sized woman. "Corey, what's up?" She nodded a greeting to Dana, who was watching gleefully, and to Steph. "Hey, Steph."

Corey looked between them. "You two know each other?"

Steph replied. "It's a small city, and when you're one of only a handful of women on the job, you tend to stick together."

"Also, we play hoops in the same women's rec league Wednesday nights," Kim added. "So, you rang?"

"Yeah." Corey nodded toward the parking lot. "That douchey, black H2 right there was driving recklessly and is parked illegally in an accessible space."

Kim nodded. "Did you see the driver?"

"Um, yes," Corey admitted. "He works here."

"So, you called me up here to ask him to move his car?"

"No." Corey shook her head. "I kind of hoped you'd make a call and have it moved for him."

Kim frowned, considering. "He deserve it?"

Dana piped up. "He deserves to be kicked in the balls twice daily."

Three sets of eyes flashed to her with no small amount of amusement and surprise.

"I'm sorry," Dana said dryly. "Did I say that out loud?"

"Did you get the plate?" Kim asked. She unclipped the radio from her belt as Steph scribbled down the plate number for her. "This is Stewart. I need Rick's Tow and Stow to the ED main entrance for a black Hummer H2 plate sierra-india-zulu-mike-tango-tango-romeo-sierra." Kim stared at the paper then rolled her eyes. The radio voice reply crackled unintelligibly to anyone but Kim, and apparently Steph, who smiled. "Copy. Out."

"What's that about his plate?" Corey asked. Kim handed her the paper and she studied it for a moment. "Size matters. God, what a dickhead."

"They should be here momentarily since they were close by. Anything else?"

"Oh, yeah." Corey pulled the pink papers from her back pocket. "Rachel's place got its liquor license and is doing concerts showcasing local artists." She handed them each a paper. "VIP passes for Friday night if you can make it. Here's one for Jules." She handed Dana an extra.

The rumble of an engine and clank of chains signaled the arrival of the tow truck and they all turned to watch right as Thayer strolled through the sliding doors.

Kim blurted. "Oh, my, god, who is that?"

"Corey?" Thayer called to her as she approached, her eyes flicking to the others in acknowledgment. "What are you still doing here? Is everything all right?"

"Oh, yeah. It's fine. We were just leaving."

"Hi." Kim stuck her hand in front of Thayer. "I don't think we've met. I'm Kim Stewart."

"Oh, right, Corey's talked about you. Congratulations on your new little one." Thayer shook her hand. "Thayer Reynolds."

Before anyone else could speak Watson Gregory III came sprinting down the hallway, bellowing in rage as he tore out the doors. "Hey. Stop. That's my car, damn it!"

Thayer's mouth quirked in amusement. "Couldn't happen to a nicer guy."

Kim smirked. "Yeah, well, you can thank Corey for—"

Corey shook her head frantically behind Thayer.

"—letting us know about the show on Friday." Kim waved her pink paper. She turned at the shouting from the parking lot. "I better go handle this." She jabbed a finger at Corey. "You owe me."

Thayer looked between the three remaining women. "Why do I get the sense I'm not in on the joke here?"

Steph covered her mouth with her hand and coughed a noise that sounded very much like a laugh. "I'll be outside."

Dana gathered up a pile of charts. "Thanks for the snacks, Corey," she called as she hurried away.

"Well?" Thayer eyed Corey.

Corey shrugged and gave her a quick peck on the cheek. "I gotta run, babe."

CHAPTER TWELVE

"Down here." Corey headed down the hallway in which two students hurried past in the opposite direction covering their mouths and noses. It was still summer so most of the offices were closed and dark but still a handful of students and staff milled about. The stench was not quite as overpowering as yesterday, but it was strong and took on a disturbing cooked quality.

Steph cleared her throat. "Yes, I guessed that." She glanced around the hallway housing the anthropology department. "Have you done this kind of thing before?"

"I have, once." Corey led them down another hallway. "The summer of my junior year. A badly decomposed man was found in his home, so Audrey was called in. It wasn't overly suspicious but there was some concern. He was found dead in his bed, but there was blood on the stairs and at the bottom landing. The door was locked from the inside."

"Who found him?"

"His local bartender. You'd have to be in a pretty committed relationship with booze for that to be the person who misses you first." She stopped outside the door to the lab to finish the story. "Anyway, it was determined the most likely scenario was that he was drunk and fell down the stairs. He had a documented history of falls and there was plenty of skeletal evidence to support that with previous healed injuries. It was assumed he made it back to his room after the fall and died there. It was ruled an accident, but there was really no way to prove if he died from a head injury or acute alcohol intoxication or something else entirely."

"This is it?" Steph gestured to the door with an 'Authorized Entry Only' sign and a dated, push button code lock on the door.

"Yeah." Corey punched in the combination.

"You know the code?"

"I picked the code. It was installed the same time we were analyzing the drunk guy." They entered the main classroom with windows that looked into a small courtyard along the opposite wall. At the front of the room was an old-school chalkboard and a large projector screen pulled down in front. Along the wall adjacent to the door were locked glass and wood, floor-to-ceiling cabinets filled with skeletons of varying sizes, ages, and ethnic origins. The floor was evenly spaced with six-foot lab tables and chairs.

Steph wandered along the cases, her face close to the glass as she studied the contents with interest. "Why did you need the extra security?"

"One night a couple of frat boys dared each other to break in and steal a bone."

"Oh, no." Steph looked at her. "Did they do any damage?"

"Only if you count puking on the floor." Corey snickered. "It was pretty funny, actually. They saw the rotten remains and hightailed out pretty quick."

"You were here?"

"Yup." Corey nodded. "Undergrads draw the overnights for these kinds of projects." She gestured toward the back of the classroom. "The lab's back here."

"You know, Dr. Marsh should really change the code once in a while."

"No one really wants to get in here that badly." She held the door for Steph as they entered the lab that spanned the width of the classroom. The air was hot and humid as two long fume hoods on each side of the room held four electric chafing dishes each and one large pot. They were all filled with steaming, muddy-brown, foul-smelling water. Between them was a large lab table covered in plastic sheeting with a few chairs around it.

Steph nodded at Officer Warren, the only other person in the room at the moment, who was leaning against the wall at the back of the room, away from the hoods. "Warren, how's it going?"

"Interesting. And boring and unpleasant. And I don't think I'll ever look at a buffet table the same again."

"I bet." Steph looked closer at the trays of human bones simmering away. "I'll take over for a while. You're to catch up with Sergeant Collier. He wants to knock on the doors of the other lake residents."

"Thanks, Austin." Warren nodded to her and Corey and then ducked out.

"Now what?" Steph asked.

A loud timer went off, startling them both.

"Time to change the water baths."

A moment later Audrey and Cin came in. "Excellent." Audrey grinned. "This will go faster."

Corey realized she was going to be put to work. "Where are all your students?"

"There's a summer seminar series. This is the last day before the semester starts. They'll be here later," Audrey explained.

"In the meantime…" Cin held out a box of latex gloves and a set of rubber tongs. "…you know the drill."

For the next several hours they removed the bones from one pan at a time with rubber tongs to avoid damaging them. The bones went onto towels over the plastic sheeting on the table and Cin worked to peel off the loosened tissue with fingertips and wood tongue depressors.

Corey helped Audrey carry each pan to the industrial biohazard sink and dump the water.

With clean water heating in the pan, Audrey went from pan to pan, adding ingredients to the water.

"What is all that?" Steph asked.

"Dish soap to degrease and meat tenderizer to break down the tissues," Audrey explained.

"And boiling water?" Steph asked surprised. "That's it?"

"That's it. But hot, not boiling. If the water boils, the bones can bounce around and break."

"How long does it take?"

"A few days." Audrey shook her head. "You don't get pristine bones over a commercial break like you see on TV. And it takes several weeks if you want them to stop stinking."

"Is there a way to do it faster?"

"Several. It all depends on what you want the bones for. There is laundry detergent that will get it done faster but it doesn't degrease. Bleach gets them nice and white. You can microwave them or boil the water like soup. That's all fine if all you want are clean bones for a museum display, for example. If you want a good trauma analysis with potential DNA extraction for identification later, you need to take greater care not to degrade them or do anything to introduce artifact and that takes time and a soft touch."

"What about a bug box?" Steph asked.

"It is a thing. But then what do you do with hundreds of biohazard bugs? It's the same reason we can't even have a window open and risk contaminating the environment."

"I understand," Steph said. "I'm hoping we don't need DNA to identify."

"I wouldn't expect so. We have a complete skeleton, and presumably, you have some idea of the possibilities for an ID. At most we'll have to use medical or dental records if necessary. Having said that, we may do an extraction anyway. It's good practice for the students."

"I see," Steph replied.

"All that slowness aside, by tomorrow morning the bones should be clean enough to lay out for a preliminary analysis. I'll be starting at nine."

Steph nodded. "I'll let Sergeant Collier know."

Corey was ready for a change when Collier came by with Kelly Warren close to dinnertime. Aside from helping to change the water baths two more times, she had sent an email to Dr. Webster updating him on the progress and letting him know of the preliminary analysis.

"How did the door-to-door go?" Steph asked.

"It was more a door, get back in the car and drive for miles and then another door. In any case the results were pretty much all the same. Don't know who lives there. Black bass boat with glitter finish. Why that's the only thing folks notice, I have no idea. We did have more luck at Jake's Bait and Tackle. Jake Butler played dumb but not very well. His name is going to come up again, I'm goddamn certain of it. A couple of the regulars confirmed it sounded like Harold Crandall's boat. Claim they haven't seen him in a while and didn't know his nephew. How's it going here?"

Steph said, "Dr. Marsh—"

"Audrey," she called from across the room.

"Audrey is going to start on a preliminary analysis tomorrow at nine."

"Good." Collier turned to Corey. "Hey, Curtis, is Doc working tomorrow?"

"Yeah, why?"

"Lillian Thayer invited me out for lunch to speak with her. I thought she'd be more comfortable with her granddaughter there."

"I'll go with you," Corey offered.

"I'm trying to put her at ease, not make her skin crawl."

"Holy shit, you should take that on the road."

"Be here all week."

"I'll have you know that Lil thinks I'm so amazing she's practically convinced I can get Thayer pregnant."

Steph laughed out loud—a lovely sound—and judging by the uncharacteristically charmed expression on Collier's face, he had never heard it and seemed to like it. He cleared his throat and stared at Corey hard. "Fine. We'll leave from here."

CHAPTER THIRTEEN

Thayer leaned against the counter at the desk, finishing the transfer orders for her last patient, discharging him to surgery. A glance at the clock told her it was nearly six and if Corey showed up within the next five minutes, she might actually be able to steal twenty minutes away to grab a sandwich and take a quick walk outside for some fresh air. She smiled to herself, feeling a flush of pleasure at the thought.

"What are you thinking about, Reynolds?" Watson Gregory sidled up next to her waggling his eyebrows lewdly.

Thayer sighed heavily and moved away from him only for him to move with her. "I bet I can guess." His voice dropped low and he put his face close enough to her ear that she could feel his breath. "It was that testicular torsion from earlier wasn't it? That got you all heated up?"

Thayer's head jerked up, and for a moment she was unsure who she was more disgusted by, him or herself for allowing it to go on. In the end she swallowed her rage and moved as far away from him as she could get and still be using the counter. "I appreciate your concern, Dr. Gregory, but I'm quite busy now." She tensed when she felt his hand slide around her waist.

"Oh, don't be like that. I was just—" He spun away from her with a shout of surprise and pain.

Thayer whirled to see Corey, blue eyes blazing fire, holding him by the thumb and torquing his hand back unnaturally. "Touch her again, asshole, and I'll break your fucking arm."

"Oh, my, god, Corey," Thayer gasped. "Let him go."

Corey gave him a shove and he staggered back gripping his wrist, his face a mask of pain.

"Dr. Gregory, I'm so sorry, are you all right?" Thayer reached for him.

Corey gaped at her. "You're apologizing to this piece of shit?"

He rubbed his wrist and glared at Corey before stalking off. "Crazy bitch."

Corey turned to Thayer. "Babe, you okay?"

Thayer's eyes darted wildly around the department. It was blessedly quiet but there were still a few patients looking their way with interest.

Her rage boiled over and she gripped Corey's arm hard and jerked her behind the wall separating the waiting patients from the view of the whiteboard.

Corey blew out a harsh breath. "That guy is—"

"Shut up." Thayer hissed and Corey's teeth clacked together in surprise. "Are you out of your mind?"

"He was—"

"Stop talking." Thayer furiously raked her hands through her hair. "You were behind his car getting towed this morning weren't you?"

Corey opened her mouth to reply but Thayer didn't give her the chance. "Don't even answer that. I already know." Thayer shook her head, her teeth grinding. "I said I would handle it, Corey. This is my place of work. How dare you come in here swinging your dick around like some jealous boyfriend?" As soon as the words were out of her mouth Thayer would have given anything to take them back when Corey went ashen and jerked back as if she'd been slapped.

Even through her glasses the hurt in Corey's eyes was a living thing and Thayer sucked in a breath, her hand going to her mouth. "Corey—"

"No," she choked out. "I got it. Sorry to bother you." She moved past Thayer rigidly.

"Corey, wait," Thayer called but she was already halfway to the door.

Thayer released a slow breath and steepled her hands in front of her face fighting tears at what she had just done. Just this morning she had described Corey as honorable, passionate, and protective, all things she loved her for, and she had just kicked her in the teeth for them.

"Dr. Reynolds, curtain three, please." Dr. Raymond Manning, the department director and her boss, materialized in front of her and handed her a chart. "And see me in my office before the end of your shift if you would."

Thayer took the chart. "Of course, sir."

Her heart pounded. She didn't even know he was here today let alone on the floor. She inhaled deeply and slammed her professional persona firmly in place as she headed to three.

"Treat 'em and street 'em, eh, Reynolds?" Dr. Gregory snarled at her as he passed in the hallway. He had seen barely a third of the patients she had.

She didn't spare him a glance and headed to the doctors' lounge to collect herself before seeing Dr. Manning. "Shit." She sighed heavily, her hands trembling. She couldn't afford an official reprimand in her file. It would seriously jeopardize her chance at a permanent position and she would have a very hard time not resenting Corey over it.

Dr. Manning's door was open so she knocked on the frame and cleared her throat, nervously.

"Dr. Reynolds, come in, please." He rose and came around from behind his desk and gestured to a chair.

She swallowed hard and took a breath before moving to take the chair. She was surprised when her boss, instead of moving back to his side of the desk, sat in the chair next to her and crossed his long, thin legs.

Thayer had no idea what direction this conversation was going to take, but she thought it best to say as little as possible until necessary.

He studied her for a moment and she thought perhaps he was using some clever interrogation technique and she worked not to visibly fidget under his gaze.

"Do you know what my nickname is?"

"Holmes."

"Yes." He smiled. "Not altogether unflattering or inaccurate however, 'All Seeing Eye' would better suit."

"I beg your pardon?"

"I see everything. I know everything that goes on in this department, whether I'm on the floor or not, whether I'm even here or not." He paused. "I know what has been going on between you and Dr. Gregory and I owe you an apology."

Thayer sucked in a surprised breath. "For what?"

"For not doing more to protect you from him."

"What? No." She shook her head. "Dr. Manning that's not your—"

"It is my job, Dr. Reynolds. I am the director of this department and have been aware of his bullying and harassment of you from the beginning. I expected you to be his mentor, knowing what was going to happen."

"How could you have known?"

Dr. Manning looked away with a strange expression of wistfulness and regret. "You know his family, of course?"

"Senator Gregory's oldest son by his third wife."

"Mmm." Dr. Manning nodded. "Watson Gregory II was a classmate of mine as an undergraduate. We weren't friends. I never had a taste for him and his ilk—spoiled, privileged, and entitled—but our paths crossed one night and he helped me out of a very unpleasant situation. The circumstances aren't important, but suffice it to say I have owed him a favor for forty years. So, when his spoiled, privileged, and entitled son was dismissed from two other residency programs, he called in that favor."

Thayer smiled humorlessly. "I'm sorry you've been put in this situation."

"It is one entirely of my own making. One I have not handled at all well, and one I have, regretfully, put you in the middle of. I had this foolish notion that working with an intelligent and accomplished woman like yourself would do the young man some good. That all said, I intend to correct my mistake immediately—beginning with you."

"Me?"

"In all other situations of personal and personnel conflict I can intervene, but ones of a sexual harassment nature need to originate with you. If you file an official complaint with me, in writing, I can submit it—"

"Wait. Wait." Thayer held up her hand. "I don't want—"

"Dr. Reynolds, you will have the full weight of this department behind you and I know you're not the only one."

"I appreciate that, Dr. Manning," Thayer smiled softly, "but I will handle this on my own. It will be more effective than a faceless reprimand from HR with mandatory sensitivity training."

His eyes narrowed at her before he barked a gravelly laugh, his eyes bright with amusement. "Somehow I knew that was going to be your reaction but I had to make the offer."

Thayer shared his humor for a moment before she grew serious. "I do appreciate your support, Dr. Manning, and I will take care of it, I assure you."

"I believe you. See that you do sooner rather than later. As enjoyable as it would be to watch Ms. Curtis get involved, if violence ensues, however warranted, I will not be able to overlook that. I would hate for her, or you, to face the fallout someone else so richly deserves."

Thayer nodded. "Yes, Corey is very protective."

"Mmm." He mused vaguely.

Thayer smiled and rose. She had nothing but Corey on her mind now and needed to go. "Thank you, Dr. Manning." She held out her hand.

"Have a good night, Dr. Reynolds." He shook it warmly. "And I'm sure I don't need to tell you this conversation is between us."

Thayer nodded. "Good night, sir."

CHAPTER FOURTEEN

Thayer stepped out of the department, her thoughts and emotions in turmoil. She wanted to find Corey, wrap her arms around her and beg her forgiveness. She knew she had hurt her badly.

She stopped when she saw Watson Gregory holding court with four of the junior residents—three men and one woman— at the edge of the parking lot. She had assured Dr. Manning she would take care of it and that's what she intended to do.

She stalked over to them, ice in her blood and fire in her eyes. "Dr. Gregory, a word please."

"Just a sec." He didn't bother to look at her as he continued with his story, clearly mocking an earlier patient.

Thayer waited patiently, schooling her mind and expression into one of serenity. This was not the first time she had to have this conversation with a male classmate or colleague but this time the stakes felt higher. This would set the tone for everyone she worked with and the other women. She owed it to herself, them, and Corey to end this, definitively.

He finally turned to her. "What can I do for you, Reynolds?"

"Stay, please." Thayer addressed the junior residents who were looking uncomfortable and making a move to leave, apparently having a good idea what was coming. "I would like you all to hear this so there is no confusion in the retelling."

Dr. Gregory widened his stance and puffed out his chest in an effort to look bigger and take up more space. "I can't wait."

Thayer trained her gaze on him. "I am a woman, Dr. Gregory." She waited a beat and, as expected, his eyes dropped to her breasts. When he dragged them back up his smug smirk was so comical Thayer almost laughed. "And a physician at this hospital."

"And?" he sneered.

"And a better physician than you in every way—and a better person." Her lip quirked in amusement as his mouth gaped. "You know it, I know it, and everyone else knows it."

"Bullshit," he spat, eyes glittering furiously.

"And you know what is the most maddening thing about that?" Thayer's gaze held his unflinchingly. "I honestly believe you have what it takes to be a great physician." His brows knit together in confusion.

"But make no mistake. If you continue to try and undermine, disparage, or disrespect me, I will make it my mission to humiliate you professionally at every opportunity. It will be far from a challenge, and I have held my tongue on multiple occasions already out of professional courtesy. I promise you if your behavior persists, I will leave you weeping alone in the men's locker room, filling out your resignation paperwork."

His smug smile had long faltered and the only resident who could still even watch was the young woman who had her hand over mouth and was staring at Thayer with wide eyes.

"I don't have to listen to this shit," he blurted, his eyes darting to the other men. They wouldn't look at him and all had varying degrees of shamed expressions—likely guilty of the same behavior at one time or another.

"One more thing, Dr. Gregory." Thayer's gaze was glacial. "If you ever put your hands on me again you better be saving my life. Are we clear?"

He could no longer make eye contact with her. "Whatever. Who's driving me to my car?" He turned to leave but no one followed. "You guys coming?"

"Nah, I'm good."

"I'm going to head home."

"Sorry, man. See you guys later."

The men dispersed in different directions and Thayer released a slow deliberate breath turning to the woman. "How was that?"

"Holy shit."

Thayer drove by Corey's condo. As cool as she was in confronting Watson Gregory, she was that anxious about seeing Corey.

Her truck was there but there were no lights on. She knocked but didn't expect an answer. Corey wasn't one to sit and brood at home. Thayer headed to the next likely place she would be. She had sent her a couple of texts but hadn't heard back from her.

It was late now and when she pulled up at Corey's gym, there was a woman locking up. Thayer headed toward the unfamiliar, older woman, possibly the owner. "Excuse me. I'm looking for Corey Curtis."

The woman looked her over, appreciatively, for a long moment. "You must be the reason she came in tonight spitting blood."

Thayer grimaced. "I'm afraid so. Did something happen?"

"You could say that." The woman snickered. "She put on quite a show looking for someone to get in the ring with her. Finally found a taker in that kid, Emma. That poor girl would do just about anything to get her attention."

"Oh, Christ, she shouldn't even be fighting yet—or ever." Thayer raked her hands through her hair. "Corey didn't hurt her did she?"

"Other way around." The woman guffawed. "She was so twisted around she must've had her head up her ass. Emma busted her nose good. Took me an hour to clean up the mess."

"Oh, no," Thayer groaned. "I just left the hospital and I didn't see her."

"Nah, you wouldn't." She shrugged. "Wiley took them all to the bar to drink their feelings."

"Perfect," she said tightly. Now Corey was going to be upset, injured, and drunk. "Thank you."

"Good luck, honey. You're gonna need it." The woman laughed as Thayer drove away.

She had been to Corey's favorite hangout a few times with her, a sports bar called The Pitch Stop, a place popular with women, one they all referred to as The Bitch. The music was good, the food was fried, the beer cold, and they could get whatever game you were interested in watching.

She didn't have to look far to see Corey belly up to the bar with a barely legal looking brunette. They were racing each other through a pint of beer followed by a shot of what Thayer suspected was tequila, while a group of women cheered them on.

"Oh, shit." Rachel turned and saw Thayer watching the display. "Hey, Thayer," she said loudly.

The women watching all gaped at her for a moment before they found something more interesting to do and drifted away, except for Rachel. The young woman drinking with Corey was pulled away by the arm by a similarly featured and equally as young looking blond friend. The blonde wore a decidedly unimpressed expression, and by the dramatic head shaking and gesticulating, appeared to be letting her know about it.

Corey straightened, wiping her mouth on the back of her hand and slammed her shot glass down on the bar. "Oh, goody, Thayer's here," she slurred nasally.

Thayer kept her expression carefully neutral and assessed her—her eyes were glassy with drink and glittering in anger. Her nose looked broken but the bones were displaced only slightly. She wasn't wearing her glasses probably because it was painful, but if she hadn't gotten a migraine from their fight or a broken nose, she was likely safe. "Can we talk?"

Corey cocked her head. "I think you said it all earlier."

Thayer considered her for a moment. "Rachel, can you get a few things for me? A clean towel, a bag of ice, a beer, and two shots of tequila. Oh, and a basket of onion rings." She handed Rachel her credit card.

"Yeah, sure," Rachel agreed.

"Thank you." Thayer nodded to an empty booth in the corner. "We'll be over there."

"I won't be," Corey sneered.

"Fine." Thayer moved over to the booth and slid in knowing Corey wouldn't stay away for long.

Rachel brought over a tray with everything she asked for while Corey sulked at the bar. "Thank you." Thayer helped herself to a shot and chased it with beer and a perfectly battered ring. "God, I needed that."

"You okay?" Rachel asked.

"It's been a day," she admitted.

"I guess." Rachel gestured to the towels and ice. "Think she's going to let you do that?"

"I don't intend to tell her." Thayer replied and popped another onion ring into her mouth.

Rachel snickered. "Can't wait to see that."

She looked past her to see Corey wobbling her way over. "Well, stick around then."

Rachel moved off while Corey clumsily slid into the booth across from Thayer and helped herself to the second shot and Thayer's beer.

Thayer took a breath. "You may be interested to hear that I put Watson Gregory III in his place after work—with witnesses. I don't expect he'll be bothering anyone again."

Corey sucked on the bottle. "Guess you put everyone in their place today, huh?"

"Corey, I am so sorry. What I said to you was vulgar and hurtful and I didn't mean it—not at all." Thayer reached across the table for her hands but Corey jerked them out of reach.

"The first two I'll give you but you sounded pretty sure of yourself."

Thayer frowned at the naked hurt on her face. "Corey, please, I'm—"

"Do you really think I would disrespect you like that? Pissing on my territory? Swinging my dick around as you so elegantly put it? That's bullshit, Thayer, and it kills me that you think that." Corey drained the beer and flagged a server down for more.

"I know, honey. I'm sorry, I am. I don't think that. It wasn't you that I was upset with. I know you were just being protective of me and you would have done the same for a total stranger. That's who you are and I love that about you. You are a righter of wrongs and I should have thanked you instead of telling you off. I know what's in your heart and you know what's in mine. So, I know you believe me when I tell you I didn't mean it and I'm so sorry. Please, forgive me." Thayer's voice cracked at the last.

Thayer saw the moment of Corey's forgiveness in her eyes. Her expression relaxed and she moved her hands across the table to reach for Thayer's. "Well, I may have overreacted a little. I just saw him touching you, and you looked really distressed. I wanted to rip his goddamn arm off. I'm sorry if I embarrassed you at work. I didn't get you in trouble did I? 'Cause I can talk to—"

"It's okay. I'm not in trouble." Thayer shook her head and laced their fingers together. "You're not the only one who overreacted. I never meant to hurt you."

Corey grinned sloppily. "Apology accepted. Forgiveness granted."

Thayer smiled gently, the weight of the day easing from her heart. "May I come sit with you and make it up to you?"

"Yes, but keep it PG. This is a family establishment."

Thayer laughed, as the bar was anything but, and slid out of her side. Corey moved over to make room for her and Thayer sat sideways in the booth so she could face her. She cupped Corey's face in her hands and placed a gentle kiss on her lips. "I love you very much." She whispered and smoothed her thumbs across her cheeks toward her nose. "Put your arms around me."

Corey did as she was told, wrapping her arms around Thayer's waist, lacing her fingers. "That's a little tender." She winced as Thayer palpated the swollen tissue.

"I know." Thayer kissed her softly again. "I'm sorry about this." She pressed her thumbs together sharply at the bridge of Corey's nose and pulled down and to the right, hearing the satisfying click as her nose realigned.

"Aw, fuck!" Corey roared, jerking back and clutching at her face with both hands as blood started to pour again, seeping through her fingers. "Thayer, what the fuck? Christ, that fucking hurt."

She winced in sympathy and reached for the towel, prying Corey's hands away and pressing it to her nose. "You'll thank me tomorrow, I promise."

"Don't fucking count on it," Corey grumbled, eyes streaming tears, and reached for her beer. "That sucked."

"Know what else would have sucked?" Rachel slid in opposite them and brought more beer. "Having to look at you and your fucked-up face without laughing for the rest of my life."

Corey glared at her and reached for the bag of ice, closing her eyes as she placed it gingerly against the bridge of her nose while holding the towel to stem the blood.

The young brunette sauntered over. "Hey, Corey. Are you feeling any better?" she purred.

Thayer was aware there was a young woman at the gym with an insatiable crush on Corey, though she had never met her. Rachel teased her about it all the time as it was somewhat of a joke.

"Emma, what's up?" Rachel asked loudly enough to get her attention. "Have you met Thayer, Corey's girlfriend?"

"Oh, hey," Emma said dismissively, her eyes flicking to Thayer briefly before training on Corey again.

"Emma, of course." Thayer nodded at the young woman Corey had been drinking with, recognizing the name immediately. "Emma of the skilled cast artwork and right hook—and apparently, high tolerance for tequila."

"It was a left jab—and mescal," she corrected snidely, as if Thayer was somehow lacking for not having known that.

Rachel coughed, her eyes darting to Thayer and then to Corey who was reddening furiously.

Corey wiped blood from her face and dropped the towel onto the table so she could talk. "Uh, yeah, better, thanks." She moved the ice pack so Emma could see. "Thayer fixed it for me."

"Well, it's good that you keep her around, I guess." Emma stretched across Thayer and stroked Corey's cheek. "It looks better already."

Rachel's jaw dropped comically, but Thayer simply arched a brow in amusement as she leaned out of the way.

"Let me know if I can do anything for you, okay, Cor?" Emma rasped suggestively. "See you, Rachel." She didn't acknowledge Thayer at all before she left.

"Cor?" Rachel snorted.

Corey placed the ice back on her face and winced, looking at Thayer from one cracked eye.

Thayer watched her walk away, extra swing in her hips, as she joined her friend across the bar whose expression was murderous. She shook her head, biting her lip to keep from laughing out loud at the young woman's brazen display. "She's cute," she said dryly, turning back to Corey.

"You're not mad?" Corey opened the other eye.

"Do I have reason to be?"

"No, absolutely hell no." Corey shook her head frantically and groaned in pain, closing her eyes.

Rachel laughed until beer came out her nose.

CHAPTER FIFTEEN

For the first time in two months Corey's splitting skull had nothing to do with her head injury. It was just a good old-fashioned hangover with a side of busted nose.

She blinked against the early morning sun filtering into her room through the cracked blinds and pushed herself higher on the pile of pillows stacked behind her. Thayer had insisted she sleep propped up to keep the swelling down and blood from pooling around her eyes as much as possible.

She gingerly touched the bridge of her nose and was surprised at how normal it felt, only hurting if she applied pressure with her fingers. She supposed she had Thayer to thank for that after all.

Thayer chose that moment to appear dressed for work with a tray of something that smelled wonderful, even to Corey's sour stomach—a breakfast sandwich, coffee, and water. "You're awake." She smiled and set the tray on the bedside table and perched on the edge of the bed. "How do you feel?"

"Like an idiot." Corey ogled the food. "Is that for me? You didn't have to do that."

"I feel badly about what happened."

"You didn't break my nose and get me drunk."

"It feels like I did."

"Come on, Thayer, I'm over it. I say and do stupid shit all the time. Last night being a perfect example. I should be making you breakfast in bed." Corey reached for her hand.

She looked down at their clasped hands. "Stupid, maybe, but never mean."

"Give yourself a break, babe." Corey tugged her fingers until she looked up. "It happened, it sucked and you made it right. Period. End of story. And besides…" Corey grinned. "… if we never fought we wouldn't have mind-blowing makeup sex to look forward to."

Thayer smiled. "Too true. Sadly, you were in no condition last night."

"Well, good thing there's like a forty-eight hour window where it still applies."

"Oh really?" Thayer arched a brow. "I hadn't heard that."

"New rule."

"That is a rule to which I will happily comply." Thayer reached for the plate. "Nana's hangover cure."

Corey examined the sandwich excitedly—fried egg, ham, and melty cheese sandwiched between two perfectly toasted pieces of bread. "With ketchup?"

"Of course." Thayer tucked a napkin in her collar.

"Mmm, amazing," Corey said around an enormous bite. "Is there any occasion your grandmother doesn't have the perfect food for?"

"If there is I have never discovered it."

"Are we going to Rachel's thing tonight?"

"Sure. If you feel up to it."

Corey nodded enthusiastically. "I'm fine."

Thayer's expression grew serious. "I don't know what your plans are today and you know I love seeing you during the day but after yesterday..."

"I'll stay away."

"Thank you."

"And speaking of Lil, I'm going with Collier to see her for lunch so he can pick her brain about the Crandalls."

"Oh, really? Whose idea was that?"

"He wanted you, but I told him you were working and that your grandmother's affection for me knows no bounds."

"Indeed," Thayer agreed. "I suspect were she fifty years younger I'd have to worry about her making a play for you."

Corey choked on her food, laughing. "Well, in case you were worried, even Lil couldn't win me away from you."

"I love you." Thayer smiled and kissed Corey's greasy lips. "I have to go. I'll see you back here later."

By the time Corey got to campus for Audrey's analysis, everyone was already there, including Dr. Randall Webster, JCMH's forensic pathologist and Corey's boss. With his overly large presence and Steph and Collier, Audrey and Cin, and the two graduate students busy laying out the skeleton on the plastic covered table, there was very little room left in the small lab.

She inched herself over to stand next to Dr. Webster to check in with her boss in person. "How's it going with your troublemaking resident in the morgue?"

"Turns out running a necrotic bowel first thing in the morning is quite humbling. He's coming around to my way of thinking." Webster's blotchy face twitched in humor. "I'm sure it hasn't been too much of a hardship for you to work with Dr. Marsh on this case?" He was well aware of her interest in forensics and skeletal analysis.

"Not at all." Corey grinned crookedly. "I haven't had the opportunity to work with Audrey in a long time so I do appreciate that." She cocked her head. "Though it has occurred to me that you're using my chosen profession as a punishment for one of your residents. Should I be offended by that?"

Dr. Webster seemed to give that some thought. "How would you feel about signing out cervical and GI biopsies on glass slides for a week?"

"Ugh." Corey rolled her eyes. "I'd rather have hot pokers jammed under my nails."

"Well, okay then." He nodded. "One person's profession is another person's penance—or something like that."

"Well said."

"Are we all set?" Audrey drew their attention to the skeleton assembled in the anatomic position on the table in front of them. The bones were stained dark, still visibly greasy and stinking, but clean of rotting soft tissue. Of note, immediately, was the stainless steel plate affixed with screws along the left femur.

The graduate students stepped back and nodded at her, but Audrey continued to stare at the skeleton. "Are you sure?"

Corey glanced around the room. Everyone was now staring at the skeleton as if expecting it to do something, and the graduate students looked particularly anxious as they were tasked with assembling it. She scanned the bones from top to bottom and back again before she saw the problem.

She waited for someone else to move and fix it, but the silence dragged on and no one else appeared to identify the offending bone yet. Steph looked amused and Collier looked annoyed at the delay.

Corey cleared her throat and stepped closer to the table, picking up a glove. "May I?"

Audrey beamed at her and gestured to the table. "Please."

Corey snapped on the glove before picking up the right fibula and turning it around, correcting the proximal and distal ends which the students had reversed. She gave the students a sympathetic smile and winked at Cin who was shaking her head and fighting a laugh.

"All right, let's get started." Audrey snapped gloves on. "This shouldn't take long." She walked to the middle of the table and picked up the pelvic girdle which was still intact, the cartilage at the joints tough enough that they hadn't given way yet so the bones could be separated. "You'll notice the pubic arch is V-shaped, the subpubic *angle* as opposed to *arch*, if you will. The pelvic inlet is smaller and heart-shaped, and the iliac crests are quite high." She looked around to see if anyone disagreed with her. "So?"

"Male." The grad students chimed in unison apparently pleased for an opportunity to make up for their earlier foible, even though it was likely everyone already knew this.

"Correct. A woman's pelvis is designed for child bearing and a man's is not—simple as that." Audrey directed her comments to the police, as they were the ones who needed the information, as she set the pelvis back on the table. "For further confirmation we can take a look at the skull." She didn't pick it up this time but pointed. "Large mastoid process, pronounced brow ridge and clearly defined external occipital protuberance—again, quite clearly male."

Audrey stayed at the skull. "Now, as for race, and I use the term loosely. We know that this is inexact at best, but based on the narrow nasal arch, narrow, curved zygomatics, blade incisors, and straight profile, I can say the man was of European ancestry."

Collier looked up from his notes and scowled.

"White," Corey supplied.

"Moving on to age. I'll be able to be more accurate once we're able to clean up the pubic symphysis, but until then, scoring the cranial vault suture fusion puts this individual as a middle adult. I would estimate late thirties or early forties. This is corroborated by the complete fusion of long bone epiphyses, the last of which—the clavicle and sacrum—occur in the early thirties." She looked around the room. "Questions so far? Okay."

Audrey moved to the middle of the table when no one spoke up. "Based on the X-rays taken at the time of defleshing, we already know there were no bullet fragments in the body and there is no evidence in the skeletal record to support his being a victim of a gunshot—or a knife wound for that matter. Does this mean he wasn't shot or stabbed? No. His wounds could have been all soft tissue injuries and that we cannot assess. However, with the absence of any blood at the scene, and I'm assuming no recovery of a bullet, I would venture to say he was neither shot nor stabbed."

Collier asked. "Any evidence of strangulation?"

"Ah, well, that's a good question," Audrey acknowledged as she picked up a thin, small U-shaped bone from near the cervical vertebrae. "The hyoid bone is intact, which does not rule out strangulation by any stretch, but it is a piece of the puzzle. If it was broken we would be having a different conversation. Dr. Webster, would you like to field this one?"

Webster cleared his throat. "If injuries were sustained from compression of the neck from manual strangulation or hanging, there would be evidence in the soft tissue. We would find bruising on the skin, ligature furrow around the neck, and petechial hemorrhaging into the eyes and skin. Additionally, there be would hemorrhage into strap muscles of the neck or damage to major vessels and infarcts in the brain tissue."

"Just to land the plane on that one, since there is no soft tissue to examine all I can say with any certainty is there is no evidence of cervical fractures to suggest trauma to the neck." Audrey paused. "At the risk of veering out of my lane and realm of expertise, and I would never swear to it in court, I would venture to say that the circumstances under which the body was found can rule out strangulation."

"How so?" Collier asked.

Audrey looked at Steph. "Officer Austin, you were down there—thoughts?"

Corey smiled to herself at Audrey never failing to take advantage of a teaching moment.

"He was a big man, presumably strong," Steph began. "It would have taken someone as strong or stronger to subdue him, assuming he wasn't already unconscious. There were no signs of a struggle inside the dwelling to suggest he was killed there and stashed under the house. It would have taken supreme effort to get a body down there. There was not a lot of room. It's also unlikely that there was a fight beneath the house where he ultimately died, and there was no evidence to support a life-and-death struggle down there."

Corey nodded, pleased to be picking up more details of the case as they went along. It was always fascinating to get all the pieces and put the final picture together. Collier's reaction was to simply grunt in acknowledgment of Steph's comments and return to scribbling in his book, but to Corey's eyes he seemed relaxed and satisfied with the information presented so far.

Audrey waited a few moments before continuing. "So, what can I tell you? There is no evidence of perimortem injury to the skull or rib cage indicating blunt force trauma, nor to the bones of the arms and hands suggesting a fight or defensive wounds. Nothing that happened to this man at the time of death involved skeletal injury. There is an antemortem record, however, that should aid in identification."

Corey bit her lip to keep from laughing as Collier looked up, interested, and flipped to a fresh page in his notebook.

"So, the obvious." Audrey gestured to the femur. "Femoral shaft fracture. Most common cause is car accident."

Corey couldn't help notice the look Steph and Collier exchanged. She could read their telepathic conversation from across the room. Edward Crandall, the owner of the property, died in a car accident and it was entirely possible his son, Robert, had been with him explaining the surgical hardware. Certainly it would be easy enough to check out.

"Any way to tell how long ago?" Collier asked.

"In adulthood, for sure. This plate is fit to this bone." Audrey picked up the bone and examined it closely. "The bone appears completely remodeled so at least a few years I'd estimate." She looked over the skeleton. "Otherwise there's not much else. Dental work which we can, preliminarily, take a look at here. If you need a more in-depth analysis, we can get in touch with a forensic odontologist. I understand you have hair for toxicology and I would encourage you to pursue that angle strongly." She shrugged. "All right, what did I miss?"

"PMI," Corey offered.

"Right, of course." Audrey shook her head. "Post mortem interval is tough here taking into account all the factors, the most critical being that the body was outside and it was warm but also dark. Insects, flies in particular, would have shown up within minutes if not sooner and accelerated what would already be happening pretty quickly in the warm weather. I have larva and pupa samples but no casings, so the life cycle was not complete. We can send them away to an entomologist and we can get a biochemical analysis on soil samples from beneath the body as well, depending on how accurate you want to get. That all takes time and money."

"Best guess, Doc?" Collier asked.

Audrey considered her answer for a long time. "Four days at a minimum and less than two weeks," she said. "Can't be more accurate than that without more testing, but I would opine time since death is closer to the four-day mark."

"Good enough for now and I totally agree." Collier snapped his book closed. "With the stench coming from that house, that body was going to be found sooner rather than later."

CHAPTER SIXTEEN

"Left here." Corey pointed to the nearly hidden entrance.

"The Pond House," Collier muttered as he drove them down the wooded winding drive to the assisted living home that Thayer's grandmother, Lillian Thayer, had moved into following a stroke that left her partially paralyzed and blind in her right eye, and unable to care for herself at home.

"Hope I get to hang in a place like this for my last days." He peered through the windshield at the enormous log cabin-style home with a wraparound front porch lined with rocking chairs that overlooked the carefully tended gardens surrounded by untouched forest. "Seems peaceful. How many residents?"

"I don't know, exactly. There are twelve suites. Some of them are doubles for couples to come together. Thayer wanted Lil somewhere that was close by and that reminded her of home."

"If Doc was coming back anyway, why didn't she just take care of her grandmother at the house?" Collier asked as he parked and stepped out into the afternoon sunlight.

"The obvious answer is Thayer's hours are too unpredictable and she's gone for long days. Lil sometimes needs more help than that."

"And the not obvious answer?"

"Well, Thayer and her grandmother are very close and very much alike. While it seems like it would have made sense for them to live together, I think they were both aware it might have jeopardized their relationship."

"Hmm," Collier grunted. "I get it."

"Oh, just a heads-up. Lil calls Thayer 'Jo' from her middle name Josephine."

"Corey." Lillian Thayer came around the side of the house. She was a tiny thing, barely over five feet, and Thayer clearly got her height from her father's side. Lil's face was creased with age and browned from the sun, her hair shock white and cut stylishly short to her shoulders. She always took advantage of the stylist team that came around twice a month and had her hair and nails done. She shuffled slightly but her steps were sure and steady as she headed for Corey. "Jo didn't tell me you were coming. Or that you got your cast off." She wrapped her arm around Corey's waist in a strong one-arm hug.

Corey returned it pound for pound, knowing despite her size and physical limitations, she was deceptively strong. "It was last minute. I just told her this morning. And the cast just came off the other day."

Lil pulled away to look up at her. "Take your glasses off for a minute and let me look at you."

Corey hesitated, knowing how this was going to go, but slid her glasses off and met Lil's gaze.

"Well." Lil's smile faltered as she studied Corey's still slightly swollen nose and the bruising beneath both her eyes, which thanks to Thayer's bar side reduction, was minimal. "I expect you'll be explaining to me over lunch how that happened."

Corey slipped her glasses back on knowing she would tell Lil everything because she would know immediately if she were lying, even by omission. "Yes, ma'am."

"And you must be Sergeant Collier." She extended her left hand as her right wouldn't grip.

"Jim, ma'am." He shook her hand with his left. "It's a pleasure to meet you, Ms. Thayer. I think very highly of your granddaughter."

"I haven't met anyone who doesn't. Call me Lillian, Jim," she replied with a smile as she looked him up and down. "Jo has never mentioned she has such a handsome friend. How old are you?"

Collier's eyes widened and he cleared his throat. "Oh, um, forty-nine, ma'am."

"Hmm." Lil frowned. "Too far outside my dating window to even consider."

Corey coughed a laugh as Collier flushed with color.

Lil, unperturbed by the exchange, gripped Corey's hand. "I've reserved a table on the patio but we must get along. There are a couple of old snakes here who would steal it without a second thought."

The view from the stone patio overlooking the large pond was lovely. There were burning citronella lamps along the railing to keep the mosquitoes away. They sat at a cloth-covered wrought-iron, umbrella table for four.

The table was set beautifully and Corey sipped on her icy lemonade and gazed out over the pond while waiting for either Lil or Collier to start the conversation. They weren't here to talk about her. Turns out she was wrong.

The serving staff came by and set a small, leafy green salad with goat cheese, cranberries and walnuts, lightly dressed with cranberry vinaigrette, in front of each of them. Corey hadn't been here for a meal in a while and had nearly forgotten how good the food was.

"So, here is what I know to be true, Corey," Lil said as she started on her salad. "I know Jo did not break your nose, and I know you have been instructed not to engage in that full contact fighting sport you enjoy, so how did that happen?"

Corey looked away, chewing her salad and strategizing a way out of a full explanation, but she felt Lil's piercing gaze on her—despite having vision only in one eye. She glanced at Collier who looked equally as interested and slightly amused. Thayer was probably not going to be happy about this as Corey was certain Lil would be addressing it with her as well.

"The other night I found out a coworker of Thayer's was…" she considered her words carefully, "…giving her a hard time."

"Say what you mean, my dear," Lil said calmly.

"Harassing her. Verbally and physically, I suspect," Corey admitted, unable to miss Collier's expression severely darkening. "I don't know the details. She didn't offer and when I asked, she told me to stay out of it and that she would handle it."

"That sounds like Jo. Go on," Lil encouraged after the server came and collected their salad plates, replacing them with small plates of assorted fruit and cheese.

"Yesterday I went over to the ED in the evening to see if she could take a break. She was at the registration counter and he had his hand on her waist." Corey's jaw clenched. "And I most definitely did not stay out of it."

Lil nodded. "Nor would I have expected you to."

"Did he hit you?" Collier asked.

"What? No. That prick? No, I removed his hand from her body."

Lil's lip twitched. "Did you remove his hand from *his* body?"

Corey shared her humor for a moment. "Not quite but he got my meaning. Anyway, Thayer wasn't nearly as appreciative of my efforts as I thought she would be and let me know with some colorfully harsh words. I won't repeat them. To be fair, I totally overstepped. And no, of course, she didn't hit me."

The server came by again to deliver the main course, a heaping plate of bacon and tomato quiche with a side of seasoned potatoes. Corey smiled at the delighted look on Collier's face, knowing he'd worried he was only going to get salad and fruit for lunch.

"So, I stormed off with my feelings hurt and went to the gym. Against medical advice, I got in the ring and being quite out of fighting form and out of my head, I got my nose broken."

"I see," Lil said. "And Jo? Have you two reconciled?"

Corey nodded and she dug into her food. "She came and found me after her shift, apologized profusely and set my nose. And this morning she made me breakfast in bed."

"And the man? Her colleague?"

Corey grinned. "I believe Thayer took care of him, as promised. Again, I didn't get the details, but if she says she put him in his place, I don't doubt it. If the tongue lashing she gave him was anything like the one she gave me, I imagine he'll be too busy licking his wounds to bother her again."

Lil nodded, seemingly satisfied for the moment. "I'll speak to Jo about it when I see her next." She looked hard at Corey. "As for you young lady, I don't expect to hear about you fighting until a doctor has cleared you to do so."

"Yes, ma'am."

They ate quietly for a few minutes. Collier had already cleared his plate. "Now, Jim. You came out here to ask me about the Crandalls. What is it you would like to know?"

CHAPTER SEVENTEEN

Corey looked up from her plate when Collier straightened in his chair and pushed his plate away before pulling his ever-present notebook from his inside jacket pocket. "I hope you don't mind if I take notes, ma'am. I find it helps me keep my thoughts in order."

"I've found the best way to retain information is to make eye contact and actually pay attention to what someone is saying." Lil smiled. "In any case, I don't have names or dates stored away, at least not ones the police wouldn't be able to discover on their own. I have impressions and feelings or memories."

Corey bit down on the inside of her cheek to keep her face neutral as Collier reddened at the gentle reprove and tucked his notebook back in his pocket. "Fair enough." His mood immediately brightened when a chocolate mousse with Oreo crumble and whipped cream served in a hurricane glass materialized in front of him. "Holy..." He pulled out the long dessert spoon, covered in goodness. "Do you always eat like this?"

Lil laughed, amused by his childlike excitement at dessert. "We do. I have a few complaints about living here but the food is not one of them. And I am not easily impressed when it comes to cooking."

Corey had never seen him look so excited with anything and made a mental note on the off chance they ever did anything nice for each other.

"While you enjoy your dessert, Jim, why don't I tell you what I remember about the Crandalls."

Corey gave Collier a triumphant smirk when Lil slid her dessert over in front of her. Lil didn't have much of a sweet tooth and Corey often benefited when they ate together.

"Albert Crandall had his property on the lake a couple of years before I purchased mine and moved out to live full time."

"He bought the land in 1973," Collier added.

"See?" Lil beamed at him. "Who needs notes?"

Collier couldn't help a smile and Corey kept her comments to herself and ate chocolate mousse to avoid getting into trouble.

"He never lived there full-time, but for many years he was at the lake every weekend to fish—even in winter. I didn't go over with a pie or anything right away. It was a little difficult to be neighborly at a distance, but we would greet each other amicably from afar if he was out in his boat."

"Was that a black bass boat?"

"Good heavens, no. It was a twelve-foot aluminum outboard." Lil laughed. "I suppose an entire year went by before I got in my own boat and went over. I had a very productive vegetable garden with way more than I could manage and no one to share it with, and honestly canning is not that much fun. As far as I could tell Albert would go out fishing all day and then come home and clean and eat his fish. I started going over to share my vegetables with him. Now, don't get excited that I know anything about him. He was a private man. He thanked me for the food, shared his catch with me if he had a good day, and we went our separate ways."

"Sometime later he started bringing his boys." Lil thought a moment. "They would have been teenagers when they started coming up, so late fifties or early sixties now."

"Edward and Harold," Jim said. "The oldest, Edward, died in a car accident a few years ago. Left behind a wife and one son of his own, Robert."

"Yes, Robert was several years older than Jo." Lil eyed him. "I don't know why you need to speak with me at all if you know all this."

Collier shrugged. "Good police work is about thorough information and evidence gathering. We don't know upfront what may or may not be important in solving a case, and you may have information which isn't a matter of public record."

"Indeed." Lil cocked her head suspiciously. "Now that you mention it, Jim, you haven't told me why all the interest in the history of the Crandalls."

"Well, ma'am, that's not really something I can—"

Corey cleared her throat to get his attention and gave him a small shake of her head to warn him off.

Collier pursed his lips. "A body was recovered two days ago from beneath the house on the Crandalls' property."

Lil's eyes narrowed. "Whose?"

"The remains were far too decomposed for identification and are being examined by our consultant forensic anthropologist."

Lil took a moment to absorb this information and sat back, staring out over the pond. "If I were a gambling woman, my money would be on Robert Crandall."

Collier blinked in surprise. "Why would you say that? It could be anyone. Someone just happening by or a transient looking for shelter."

"The information on the Crandalls was the first thing you researched, correct?"

Collier nodded. "Of course."

"Have you located Robert yet?"

"No," he admitted after a moment. "Or Harold."

Corey had remained silent long enough. "You don't seem surprised. Why would you think that, Lil?"

"After Albert stopped coming out, I suppose he was too old or too sick, Harold really spent the most time out at the lake. Then when Robert was old enough, he started joining his uncle. I paid particular attention because by then Jo was spending her summers with me and they were close enough in age that I thought it would be good for her to have a friend out here. She had Dana when we went into town or when Dana's mother dropped her by for a play date, but she didn't have anyone else even close to her own age. I knew immediately, however, a relationship with my granddaughter and that young man was never going to happen."

"She and Robert didn't get along?" Collier asked.

"I never even introduced them." Lil's eyes darkened. "In fact, I did everything in my power to ensure they never crossed paths. Jo has always been a beautiful, kind, and thoughtful girl, and Robert, even separated by a few hundred yards of water, was trouble. And I don't mean smoking a joint behind the house or nicking a bottle of booze, although I'm sure there was plenty of that too."

Both Corey and Collier were listening intently and Corey could tell from the way his fingers were drumming excitedly on the tabletop that he was itching to get his notebook out.

"Please, go on, Lillian." Collier used her name for the first time.

She inclined her head slightly in apparent approval. "He was an abuser of animals."

Collier looked perplexed. "I don't follow."

"He had a pellet gun. When he was younger, he would sit out and shoot at whatever small critter, squirrel, rabbit, chipmunk, skunk even, had the misfortune of getting within his line of sight."

"That's not so unusual."

"If he didn't kill them right off—and I'm all but certain he wasn't trying to—he would build a fire and burn the poor wounded creatures alive or devise some horrible contraption with a cage and a pulley strung up over the water to drown them over a period of hours."

"Jesus Christ," Corey blurted. "Little fucking psycho."

"Corey," Lil admonished, without heat.

Collier frowned. "How do you know this? You couldn't see them from across the lake."

"With binoculars you can see quite clearly. The property wasn't nearly as overgrown as it is now. I didn't set out to snoop, but I admit, I was curious about the boy, and when I started hearing the shots—sound travels across water like you're standing right next to someone—well, I snooped."

"Where was Harold Crandall in all of this? For that matter, where was the boy's father, Edward?"

"I suspect Harold was fishing. He had the taste for it like his father before him. As for Edward he was probably home with his wife crying, praying or drinking about how they bore such a soulless little monster. I always wondered if Harold took Robert under his wing because they were more like minded."

Corey's eyes widened. She had never heard Lil speak so harshly about someone. "And Thayer never met him?"

Lil blinked, considering. "She did once, though she may not remember. She was maybe six or seven. Robert would have been a young teenager. I took her into town to see a film at Tower Theater. She was very excited. We bumped into Harold and Robert. Harold remembered me from the times we had met before when he was younger and stopped to chat. Robert was outwardly polite and pleasant but his eyes held the truth—cold and cruel. They were going to the movies as well and my skin simply crawled at the idea of even being in the same building with them and breathing the same air."

"What happened?" Corey asked.

"Nothing." Lil pressed her lips together thinly. "I told Jo I was getting a headache and didn't think I could sit through a loud, bright movie and promised I would take her another day if we could go out for hot dogs and ice cream instead. She was very disappointed but she understood."

Collier nodded, his expression tense. "I appreciate your thoughts and recollections, Lillian, but how does it explain why you think the body is Robert Crandall?"

Lil gazed across the pond for a moment before turning her attention back to them. "He was without a doubt a bad seed and destined to die horribly. I hope he did."

CHAPTER EIGHTEEN

They had managed to turn the conversation to more pleasant topics before they left. Lil took them around to walk off some of their lunch and showed them the work she had been doing in the gardens.

They had parted warmly with promises to visit again soon and Lil even extended an invitation to Collier to come back and bring a date. He reddened and insisted there was no special someone, while she eyed him, clearly not believing a single word. Corey wasn't certain she believed him either.

"I can hear the rusty gears turning in your head," Collier said into the silence on the drive back to campus. The first half of the drive he spent on the phone—first to Steph, telling her to expect him back on campus, then ordering Kelly Warren to meet him there, and finally to an officer named Taggart to take over skeleton sitting duties.

Corey gave herself a small shake and continued to stare out the window. "I'm just having a hard time wrapping my head around the way Lil described that boy, Robert. It was chilling. Thayer is very much like her grandmother. She's warm, caring, has a huge heart and sees the good in everyone. She can find humor in everything. Hearing Lil refer to someone as a soulless monster surprised me just as much as if Thayer had said it."

"You don't believe her?"

"Oh, no, I absolutely do. That's what's so disturbing."

"With all due respect, is there any chance Lillian isn't all there?"

Corey snorted. "Besides Thayer, Lil is the most level-headed and put together person I know. I obviously didn't know her before the stroke, but Thayer tells me if she didn't know better, she would say Lil is sharper now—perhaps due to her physical disabilities."

"Hmm," Collier grunted.

"More importantly, what are you thinking?"

After a long moment he said, "I think it's time to pay Edward's widow and Robert's mother a visit."

Corey didn't comment, but based on the physical assessment, she couldn't see how the body could be anyone but Robert Crandall at this point. Lil's opinion, while not evidence, certainly supported that assumption. They pulled into the parking lot outside the anthropology building where Steph and Officer Warren were waiting for them. Collier made no move to get out of the car.

"The asshole giving Doc a hard time—his name Gregory, by chance?" he asked, his gaze trained out the windshield.

"Yeah, why? You know him?"

"Of him. The department got word he was coming into town. There was talk of a joint security detail but he refused. Wouldn't have involved me, but I overheard his name the other day in conjunction with a shit ton of unpaid parking violations. Thought nothing of it until a call was made to the brass and his slate was cleared. Spoiled pricks like him give me the shits."

"Yeah, that's him." Corey breathed a laugh. "I had his car towed yesterday morning from an accessible spot at the hospital."

Collier barked a laugh. "Good for you."

"Not when Thayer found out."

"You want me to step in? I'd be happy to have a word with him."

Corey was touched but smiled grimly. "Would you be happy being on the business end of a Thayer Reynolds dressing down?"

"Not even remotely." He paused. "But I would do it if you asked."

"Thank you, but on behalf of both of our lives I appreciatively decline."

"Thank Christ."

Corey joined them in the parking lot, interested to hear what their next moves were going to be.

"How was lunch?" Steph asked.

"Delicious," Collier said. "And interesting."

Steph arched a brow in his direction but waited for him to explain.

"You ready to go talk to Robert Crandall's mother?" he asked.

"Are you ready to ID him as the deceased to her?" Steph asked.

"Not quite, but that's the direction we're heading. There's been no activity on his cards for a week, no one has reported him missing, and no one has seen him. And we need to know more about Harold Crandall and find him, too, and she's the only connection we have."

Kelly Warren asked, "What about me, Sarge?"

"I want you to get me a list of unsolved crimes in the city with available but unmatched DNA evidence. Everything—assaults, arson, theft, whatever."

Corey fought a laugh as Officer Warren pulled out a little notebook like Collier's and started scribbling. "Going back how far?"

"Thirty years." Officer Warren's head jerked up and Steph looked at him with surprise. "And talk to Oneonta PD. That's where the Crandalls' permanent residence is. None of them show up as having a record except for traffic violations but I want to know more. Were they ever liked for anything? And see if you can get some departmental help in locating Harold. We don't want to step on any toes. If they give you a hard time have them call me. Oh, and get me Robert and Harold Crandall's prints. They've got to be on record somewhere."

Only Corey frowned at him with some semblance of understanding. "You're thinking Robert Crandall has never been caught?"

"One thing at a time, Curtis. But if what Lillian Thayer described about his behavior is true, animal cruelty is where it started, not where it ended. You have a job too. Let Dr. Marsh know I'll be getting a warrant for medical and dental records for our most likely ID and she'll have them by the end of the day. And find out how fast she can do a DNA analysis on the bones and what it will cost. I'll work on getting the department to pay for it."

"I wouldn't worry too much about that." At Collier's questioning look she explained. "If anything comes of the DNA analysis, there are probably a handful of grad students that could get a publication out of it. Someone's grant money will foot the bill." Corey offered him a mock salute and headed into the building.

CHAPTER NINETEEN

Thayer shivered slightly as they stood in line outside the Old Bridge Coffee House. The days were still warm but once the sun set, they were reminded fall was just around the corner. She knew it would be hot inside with all the people they were packing in and she dressed in jeans and a sleeveless top. She was beginning to regret her insistence on waiting in line with everyone else instead of waving their VIP passes like others were doing to gain immediate entrance.

She took her mind off the chill by reading the nearby sandwich board that explained fifty percent of the cover was going to the musician and the other fifty was going to the local SPCA. It was clear why Rachel's business was so successful. She knew her audience. Thayer nudged Corey and pointed to the sign. "Check that out."

Corey peered around her to read it. "Oh, that's crafty. Who doesn't want to save the puppies? And she'll make twice the door take in booze and food."

"Mmm." Thayer ran her hands over her arms to warm them.

"Here, babe." Corey slipped off her sweatshirt and draped it over Thayer's shoulders.

Thayer didn't bother trying to protest and pulled the hoodie around her. It was warm from Corey's body and smelled like her soap. Corey, with the high metabolism of the extremely fit, was a walking heater. Thayer looked at the garish, colorful patterns across the black sleeves of the sweatshirt and smiled to herself at the memory it evoked.

The first time Corey took Thayer to The Pitch Stop, an informal dyke sports bar, a pack of rowdy, gym-tan-laundry bros had come in. Why was anyone's guess, either as a joke or because they were lost. They proceeded to get drunk, insult the servers, and offend the other patrons with their crude bigotry.

Corey and Rachel had leaned across the bar, laughing maniacally, and switched every television in the bar from the live games to whatever talk show and soap opera rerun they could find. The other women caught on and the room grew quiet as they all found a table and pretended to watch the shows in earnest, going so far as to shush each other if someone spoke.

The men protested loudly and profanely before throwing cash on their table and leaving to gales of laughter and cheers. Jan, the owner, bought a round for the house. It was hilarious and though they had been weeks away from saying the words, Thayer fell a little deeper in love with Corey at that moment. As a joke Thayer bought her a sweatshirt like the ones the men were wearing, but the joke ended up being on her when it became Corey's new favorite article of clothing and she wore it everywhere.

She leaned into Corey and slipped her arm around her waist, wanting to feel their bodies touching. Corey draped her arm across her shoulders and pulled her close.

"Are you okay?" Corey asked.

"Very," Thayer sighed, her whole body warming at the contact. "I'm very happy and very much in love with you."

"Even after I ran my mouth to Lil about what happened with your coworker?"

Corey had returned to the condo in plenty of time to make dinner for them. That meant cheeseburgers on the grill, salad from a bag, and tater tots from the freezer. She wasn't much of a cook but her dedication to comfort food and token vegetables was appreciated. Thayer was always an enthusiastic eater, especially if she didn't have to make it.

They had talked over dinner. Watson Gregory had switched his shift out with another fourth-year resident, and for the next few days when she was off, Thayer wouldn't even see him.

The news of her conversation with him had spread like wildfire and she hadn't failed to notice the appreciative nods from many of the female staff—some of the male ones too.

Corey told her about her lunch date with Lil and Collier, and they had a good laugh about Lil's teasing and flirting with him. Thayer remembered the day they were going to the movies when she was little but didn't recall meeting Harold and Robert Crandall. She shuddered when Corey recounted her grandmother's description of Robert, grateful she couldn't remember.

"Oh, come on." Thayer looked up at her. "You really think Nana wouldn't have wormed the situation at work out of me?"

"Well, yeah, but it was your story to tell."

"It was yours too." Thayer gave her waist a squeeze. "Anyway, she was probably more upset about me lashing out at you than she was about me being sexually harassed at work." Thayer could feel Corey's rumbling laugh through her chest.

"With any luck she'll make you apologize to me again." Corey kissed Thayer's temple. "Your makeup sex game is strong."

"Rivaled only by yours." Thayer smacked her on the ass. "It's too bad we get along so well. We could be doing it like that all the time."

They were both cracking up when they finally reached the front of the line and the smiling, dimpled Jude who was taking the cover and stamping hands for those over twenty-one. "You know you two didn't actually have to wait in line," he commented as Corey held out two twenties. "Or pay."

Corey grinned. "It's for the puppies."

"Have fun ladies." Jude took the money. "Your table is near the front window."

"Our table?" Corey arched a brow at Thayer as they finally entered the already crowded and warm room. There were at least a hundred people milling around and chatting in small groups with beer, wine, and snacks.

The tables were full and Corey noticed the back where the ratty sofa and chairs usually lived had been converted to a small raised stage lit with floor spotlights. There was a stool, table, microphone and amplifier set up. A couple of guitars rested in their stands.

"Corey, Thayer," Jules called to them from near the window. "Over here."

"Our table." Thayer pointed at the two high tops that had been pushed together and the handful of tall chairs. There was a bucket of ice and a bottle of wine and several beers already on the table, and nestled between them a hot pink sign marking the tables as reserved.

Corey's eyes widened at the star treatment Rachel had rolled out for them. She nodded to Dana and Jules who were talking animatedly and gesticulating with wineglasses wildly enough that she suspected they had been emptied and filled more than once already.

"Want something?" she asked Thayer as her hand hovered over the table.

"Wine, please." Thayer had moved over to the other side to greet her friends while Corey poured her a glass and handed it across the table. "Thank you."

Corey returned her loving gaze, for a moment thinking seriously about leaving and taking Thayer back home for some more quality alone time. She took several long swallows of her beer and shook herself out of her libidinous thoughts.

"Listen up, bitches." Rachel's voice boomed from the microphone as she took the stage. "For those of you who don't know, I am Rachel Wiley and I'd like to welcome you all to our first charity and local artist concert series."

"You need a better name!" someone heckled jokingly from the crowd.

"Yeah, no shit," Rachel agreed. "You know what? Drop your suggestions off at the counter. Winner gets two VIP passes for September's concert."

Corey's eyes widened as the crowd cheered loudly and whistled. Rachel was full of surprises. Up until now, because Rachel had wanted to keep a low profile, Corey had never really seen her work.

"Before we get started with the music, there are a few housekeeping things to get out of the way." She trained her gaze to the front door and Corey looked where she was staring. Jude closed the door and made a slashing motion across his throat. "So, we have a full house tonight, which is fucking outstanding. In the event of an emergency there is the front door and…" she hooked a thumb behind her, "…another exit through the kitchen and storeroom in the back."

"Next, in case you missed it, all door proceeds will go to either the musician or the SPCA." She paused for the clapping again. "Over by the counter there is a table set up where Cam will be selling CDs and other swag. If you like what you hear tonight, let her know by supporting her work. Also, there is a table with a couple of boxes. We are taking requests and suggestions for future artists to perform and also for charities you would like to see supported. So make your way over at some point tonight and let us know what you think."

"Finally, this is an all-ages show. Those of age may purchase wine and beer and I encourage you to do so. Those not of age, may fucking not. It's as simple as that. If you get caught by me or my staff drinking underage or supplying drinks to someone underage, you will be summarily dismissed from my house with my boot in your ass and banned for life. For those of you over twenty-one, have a great time, but keep in mind this is not a sports bar so let's keep it respectful and classy." Rachel scanned the crowd until her eyes found Corey's. "I'm looking at you, Corey."

Corey choked on her beer and looked around, panicked as people turned to stare at her, disapprovingly.

"I'm just kidding, dude." Rachel laughed. "All right, enough about me and you. Old Bridge is thrilled to introduce hometown gal, Cam Delmar. She's got one album out and working on some new stuff and we're very pleased she could join us tonight. So, let's hear it for her."

Rachel stepped back from the microphone and Cam stepped out onto the stage. The lights dimmed while the crowd clapped and whistled. She was super cute with blond pixie hair and elfin features. She wore tight jeans and a plain white V-neck shirt, not at all what Corey expected given the powerful, throaty voice she had heard through the speakers the other day.

"Thank you, Rachel," Cam said as she took the stage. "Thank you guys for coming out tonight. Let's get this party started." She settled the guitar strap across her shoulders and grinned broadly.

Rachel made her way over to the front of the shop, greeting people along the way as Cam Delmar rocked out. Her talent on the guitar was amazing, her voice strong, and she looked like she was having a blast as the crowd moved with the rhythm of her music.

Rachel smiled at Corey. "Glad you could make it."

"You're an asshole." Corey tried to glower at her but couldn't pull it off.

"Yup." Rachel gestured to her tinted glasses. "You don't need those in here, do you?"

"No." Corey shrugged. "I just didn't want to answer a lot of questions about my busted face."

"How is this busted any different from your usual *busted*?" Rachel gave her a gentle shove.

Corey shook her head. "You know you're really good at this." She gestured vaguely around the room.

"I know. Nice of you to notice."

"No, I just mean…" Corey struggled to put it into words. "…you know, I've never seen you be open and proud of your accomplishments. You always wanted to be in the background. Center stage is a good look for you."

Rachel smiled, eyes dancing. "Dude, are you hitting on me?"

"Not until you look at me like that." She nodded at Thayer, who was watching their conversation from across the room. Her eyes sparkled and she smiled seductively when Corey met her gaze.

Rachel gave Thayer a wave. "Jesus, that woman is unearthly. Sometimes I can't even look at her." She turned back to Corey but her eyes were drawn to someone coming in through the door and her face sobered. "Uh-oh. I better see what's up."

Corey followed her gaze and put a hand on her arm when she saw the uniformed officer. "She's cool. That's Collier's new partner. I invited her."

"That's Collier's partner?" Rachel's eyes widened. "Good on him."

CHAPTER TWENTY

Steph looked exhausted. Her uniform was far less crisp than that morning, her eyes less alert and her usually smooth bun was coming out in wisps around her face. "You're not still on duty, are you?" Corey asked.

"Yes and no," Steph said. "I have to put in a few hours over on campus in a bit so Collier can go over old cases with Warren. If I go home I'll never get back out again, so I thought I'd stop by."

"Jesus, when do you sleep?"

"I caught a nap in the car on the way back from Oneonta."

"That's like an hour away, tops."

"Compliments of the house." Rachel appeared with a large to-go cup of coffee and set a basket of sweeteners and creamers on the table within reach and a wax paper-wrapped sandwich. "It's turkey."

Steph groaned. "God bless you."

"Steph Austin, this is Rachel Wiley, my best friend and owner of this dump."

"Nice to meet you, Rachel." Steph extended her hand. "Congratulations on your 'Best Of' wins."

"Thank you." Rachel shook her hand. "You read the article?"

"Actually, Sergeant Collier mentioned it. Told me he knew you," Steph explained and sipped her coffee. She smiled when Corey's mouth gaped and Rachel's eyes bulged from her head. "What?" Steph asked, looking between them.

Corey laughed and hid behind a swallow of beer, eyeing Rachel merrily.

Rachel shrugged. "Jim Collier walked in on me going down on his son back in college. That's how we, ahem, met."

Steph blinked for a moment before throwing her head back in laughter. She laughed for a long time, wiping tears from the corners of her eyes.

"I'm so sorry." Steph gulped a breath and got herself back under control. "I'm sorry, I'm not laughing at you, Rachel, I promise." She hiccupped. "I can imagine the look on his face, oh, my god."

"It's cool," Rachel agreed. "It was funny, then. It's still funny. Imagine my surprise when it turns out Corey's his work wife. Our paths cross occasionally as a result."

"I'm his what?" Corey spluttered, beer dribbling down her chin.

"You heard me," Rachel shot back. "You two squabble like an old married couple."

Steph nodded in agreement while Corey shook her head in emphatic denial.

Rachel looked up at the stage as Cam started talking about taking a break for a few minutes. "Oops. I should be paying better attention. I gotta go mingle. Nice to meet you, Steph. Stop in anytime and bring Collier. Coffee is always on me."

"Thanks." Steph gave her a wave as Rachel disappeared into the crowd.

Once the music was off Corey no longer had to raise her voice to be heard. "So, tell me about Oneonta." She opened another beer and peered around for Thayer, who had worked her way forward and was at the tables with Dana and Jules, writing suggestions for charities and other local artists to perform.

"You know you're not actually investigating this case, right?" Steph asked as she unwrapped her sandwich.

"Come on," Corey encouraged. "We recovered a decomp together. That's gotta count for something."

"It does. I have a profound respect for you and what you do and I hope you're a new friend. But it doesn't make you a cop," Steph denied her gently. "Why do you even want to know?"

"I'm already in the loop and I just want to see it through to the end, and personal interest, I guess." Her eyes flicked to Thayer wending her way back over to them through the crowd.

Steph followed her gaze. "She doesn't have anything to do with this. I know it hits close to home—literally."

Thayer slipped her arm around Corey's waist giving her a gentle kiss on the mouth. "You two look serious." Thayer looked between them. "Everything all right? Steph, are you here officially?"

"No." Steph smiled. "Just passing time and enjoying some real life and excellent coffee before I have to go back to work."

"Well, it's nice to see you again. I'm glad you decided to stop by."

"Thank you." She nodded at the door. "I'm going to listen to as much as I can over there so I can make a quick getaway."

"Are you having a good time?" Corey asked when Steph had left.

"Yes." Thayer smiled and leaned into her as the music started up again.

Corey draped her arms over Thayer's shoulders and pulled her close against her, back to front. Thayer swayed gently to the music and Corey slowly stepped them backward closer to the front window and away from the people so they had more room and more privacy. "Are you all done schmoozing for the night?" Corey asked, her lips close to Thayer's ear.

Thayer turned and kissed her softly. "I only want to schmooze with you."

"Mmm, that is a slippery slope." She brushed Thayer's thick auburn curls from the back of her neck and kissed along behind her ear as she shivered. "I've read schmoozing is a gateway to canoodling."

"Oh, no." Thayer laughed and tilted her head, granting Corey better access to her neck. "What happens then?"

Corey nipped her sensitive skin and heard Thayer's breath hitch. "Canoodling leads inevitably to only one thing." In the darkened room she made a bold move and ran her hands down Thayer's chest and over her belly. She tucked her fingertips down the waistband of her jeans. "Nooky."

Thayer shook with silent laughter and gripped Corey's forearms holding her in place. Corey could feel Thayer's heart thudding through her back.

She heard Rachel talking loudly to the room from nearby and saw from the corner of her eye when she stood on a stool. She heard wild applause. She heard Cam Delmar thank Rachel and the audience and tell a story about her grandmother and the music she played for her and one of her greatest influences— Joni Mitchell.

The last song started, "A Case of You." Corey had heard the song but never really listened to the lyrics before.

Thayer began to move again, singing softly, her hips and ass pressing against Corey, heating her blood.

Corey spun Thayer in her arms, her right arm slipping around her lower back and her left cupping around her neck as Thayer's arms slid around her waist.

She was only dimly aware of the one hundred other people in the room, of Rachel standing and swaying on the stool a foot from her. Her senses were filled with the music and the warmth and smell of the woman in her arms. Thayer's hands were at her waist and head on her shoulder, her hair tickling her face. Corey was completely lost, her mind and body suffused with love.

She felt Thayer tense in her arms, her head coming up sharply. "Babe?" She pulled away slightly to look at her, seeing a worried frown crease her brow as she stared over Corey's shoulder. "What's wrong?"

Thayer's expression darkened. "There's a bunch of kids out on the sidewalk..." She paled. "Corey..."

Corey spun in time to see a flurry of movement outside the window a split second before the plate glass window shattered. It happened in an instant and time stood still. She saw Rachel spin off the stool with a shout and disappear from her peripheral vision. She enveloped Thayer in her arms and used her full height to cover her, hunching them over and making them as small as possible while the splintering glass exploded, raining thick shards across her back.

It was over in seconds. Voices were loud, shouting and crying as the lights came up. The floor was covered in glass shards and several bricks thrown through the window.

Corey straightened and pulled Thayer up with her. "Are you all right?" She looked her over, face pale and golden eyes dark but she could see no sign of blood. "Thayer, are you cut?"

Thayer met her eyes finally and gave herself a shake. "No. No, I'm okay." Thayer looked worriedly back at her. "Corey, you're bleeding."

She felt the sting now on the side of her neck. She touched her fingertips to the area and they came away tipped with blood. "It's okay. It's nothing."

"Thayer, I need you," Dana called from nearby. She was on the floor crouched next to Rachel who appeared dazed, blood streaming from multiple cuts to her hands and arms.

"Jesus." Thayer pulled away from Corey. "Someone get some towels and call an ambulance."

Static crackled near Corey's ear and Steph materialized out of nowhere, her hand gripping the radio handset at her shoulder, shouting orders for backup and ambulances at their location.

"We've got multiple assailants...on foot running east... officer on scene."

Corey's head snapped up at the sound of high-pitched, cackling laughter from the street, profane shouts and the pounding of running feet.

Rachel was sitting up. Thayer and Dana pressed blood-soaked towels to her body. Jules held a wad of napkins to the arm of another woman.

Corey was overcome with white-hot rage as she looked around at the chaos and fear. In the next instant she tore through the door, shouldering through people trying to leave.

"Corey, no!" Steph yelled behind her as she hit the street at full stride, the whining sickly laughter of the punks responsible ringing in her ears.

CHAPTER TWENTY-ONE

Half a block down Corey saw the group of them flash beneath a streetlight. It was past midnight and there were few people out and traffic was light. She veered into the middle of the street and put on a burst of speed as she gained ground. They weren't expecting a foot pursuit and were loping down the sidewalk, laughing and gloating, shoving each other around, their garbled voices talking over each other.

One of them must have looked back and seen her. "Oh fuck, man. Go! Go!"

Together they broke into a sprint and turned down a narrow one-way street. Corey heard a shrill horn and the squealing of tires over the sound of her own labored breathing and blood pounding in her ears. She took the corner, skidding out of the way, her hands slamming against the side of the car which had slowed to a crawl after their near miss with the vandals. The horn blared again, and the driver shouted expletives out the window at her as she regained her footing and kept on, hearing the slapping of feet, and panicked laughter up ahead.

She pinballed down the alley between the Laundromat and Shawarma Shack and skidded to a stop, breathing hard, her ribs and shoulders aching with the effort.

The alley was closed off by an eight-foot, rusty, chain-link fence. Three figures stood on the other side yelling, "Come on! Come on!" as two others dropped to a dumpster and then to the ground on the debris-littered pavement.

A sixth man straddled the top of the fence and she met his leering and laughing gaze. He had a ratty complexion and lank, greasy, brown hair hanging over his face, which couldn't hide his malicious eyes glittering in triumph.

They stared at each other a long moment. Corey was fixated in rage at their violation, completely unaware that the others were arming themselves with debris from the alley.

The lank-haired man flipped her off with a laugh before dropping to the ground as his buddies let loose. Multiple bottles and brick shards sailed over the fence. She registered the danger a split second before a hard body slammed into her, crashing her against the brick wall, covering her, as bottles popped and exploded where she had been standing.

It was over in a moment, the night now filled with sirens, red and blue lights flashing through the alley, shouts and booted feet running.

"Corey? Are you all right? Are you hurt?" Steph shouted at her between panting breaths as she eased her weight off her and moved away from the wall.

"What?" Corey stared, blinking at her, her heart pounding. "I'm fine."

"Jesus Christ." Steph gasped, her hands going to her knees while she took deep breaths.

Corey stepped away from the wall and strode to the fence. "They went that way."

"No shit." Steph straightened.

Corey whirled around. "Are you just going to let them get away?"

Steph's eyes narrowed and she stalked toward Corey, eyes blazing. "Are you insane? They could be armed. You could have been hurt or shot. My job is to protect. That means you." She jabbed Corey in the chest with two fingers, staggering her. "What the hell was I going to do? Draw my weapon and watch you get showered in broken glass and bricks? Fuck."

"Austin!" Collier strode down the alley, now well-lit with patrol cars. "Report."

Steph eyed Corey and took a shuddering breath. "Let's go."

Corey followed them out of the alley back to the street abuzz with officers, radios crackling into the night. She figured she was three blocks from the Old Bridge and turned to head back there, Steph and Collier a few yards ahead of her.

Collier turned to glare at her, his eye twitching wildly, his anger clear. He listened to Steph's report with one ear while barking orders to the officers as he went by.

Corey saw the ambulance lit up with doors open. Rachel was being loaded into the back, joking about something with Dana and Jules on either side while Thayer spoke to the paramedics. She exhaled a relieved breath at seeing them all okay. There was a crowd on both sides of the street and a few police officers ushered them back and urged them to disperse.

She started to move toward Thayer when a hand like iron closed around her upper arm and spun her into a car parked at the side of the road.

Hands pressed into her back, forcing her up against the car. She held out her own hands to stop herself from going face first over the hood.

"Corey Curtis," Collier growled as he kicked her legs apart and pressed her against the hood. "You are under arrest."

"What?" She attempted to straighten but was held down by a large hand between her shoulder blades. "Collier, what the fuck?" she yelled as his hands roughly patted across her shoulders, down her back and up and down each leg. He removed her phone and wallet from her back pockets before a hand snaked around her head and pulled the glasses off her face.

"For interfering with an arrest, disturbing the peace, and public intoxication. You have the right—"

"Are you fucking kidding?" Her right arm was twisted behind her and she heard the clink of metal and felt the bite of a cuff ratchet around her wrist.

"—to remain silent. Anything you say can be used against you in a court of law. You have the right to an attorney. If you cannot afford an attorney, one will be appointed for you. Do you understand your rights?"

He jerked her left arm behind her and Corey arched back off the car with a hiss of pain, her already taxed ribs screaming in protest, as he secured her other wrist. "What the hell, Collier?"

"Corey?" Thayer's voice rang out over the others.

Corey was spun around and she saw Thayer watching, confusion and worry etched on her face. Steph stepped in front of her, keeping her at a distance. The look on Steph's face was a mix of steely resolve and deep sympathy.

"Do you understand your rights?" Collier repeated as he propelled her toward his car.

"Yes," Corey said through clenched teeth, swallowing her fear and pain while Collier opened the passenger door and pressed her in.

"What the hell is going on? Why is she being arrested?" Thayer yelled, uncaring who saw her distress. "Steph, please." Thayer tried to move past her but Steph gripped her arm and put her body in front of her.

"Thayer, don't," Steph warned. "You'll make things worse."

"Worse?" Her eyes filled and she could see Corey's tension and pain as Collier bundled her into the car.

"I'm sorry," Steph said softly. "It wasn't my call. He's angry and—"

"Angry? Who here isn't angry?"

Steph shook her head and sighed heavily. "I'll drive you to the station."

Thayer nodded, running her hands down her arms, feeling the softness of Corey's sweatshirt she'd had the foresight to put back on before coming outside. She heard Corey's keys jangle in the pocket. "No. I'll drive myself. I need to go back to the condo first."

Thayer pulled into the station close to an hour later, her heart hammering with dread and fury at what had happened. She had already called the hospital. Rachel was okay. There had been a lot of blood but only a few of the cuts on her hands and arms needed suturing. She was being released shortly, and Dana and Jules were taking her back to the shop to inspect the damage and make sure it was secure, and then home.

Thayer slung her purse over her shoulder and headed into the station, an older four-story gray building in standard bland government style. She had never been inside. She had never had a reason. It was past one in the morning now, but she didn't feel tired, only anxious, angry, and desperately worried about Corey.

She stopped at a long front reception desk, protected by a Plexiglas window and manned by a bored, older officer in uniform. She didn't wait for him to acknowledge her. "I need to speak with Sergeant Jim Collier immediately."

The man looked up, eyes narrowed at the demand, apparently bristling at being told what to do. "He's busy."

"He'll see me. Please, let him know Thayer Reynolds is here."

The officer's eyes widened slightly and he stared at her curiously for a moment before nodding. It occurred to her that though they had never met, he might have recognized her from the incident at the construction site. Either that or Jim had told him to expect her.

The officer picked up the phone and jabbed in the number. "Sarge, Thayer Reynolds is here to see you." He watched Thayer as he listened a moment. "Right away, sir." He was buzzing her in before the phone was back in the cradle. "Through the door and up to the second floor, ma'am. He'll meet you."

Thayer worked to steady her breathing and slow her racing heart as she topped the stairs to a landing with dark hallways to the right and left and double doors in front of her leading to a large, brightly lit room. She saw Collier heading toward the doors from the other side and pushed through them before he reached her.

She glanced around at the two dozen desks pushed together in pairs, facing each other making desk squares all over. A few were occupied with plainclothes cops she assumed were detectives. A couple of men glanced her way but paid her no other mind. She wondered if this was a specific division—homicide, narcotics, or vice. She was just rattling off words in her head she'd heard on television. She had no idea how the department worked or what Jim Collier was the sergeant of. Right now she didn't care.

"Where is she?" Thayer asked him tightly.

"Come with me." He gestured for her to follow.

The back wall was a line of offices, all of them dark but one, and for a moment she thought that was where they were headed but he veered off to the side. Apparently, he wasn't high ranking enough to have an office with a door, but he did rate a pair of desks somewhat removed from the others with a partial wall separating it from the larger room.

Thayer expected to see Corey at his desk and was dismayed to find the space empty but for the desks and chairs and one visitor chair he indicated she should take. She sat and he settled himself back at his desk.

"Where is she?" Thayer demanded again.

"Being processed."

"Processed?" Thayer stiffened. "Do I need to call a lawyer?"

"Look, Doc—"

"You may call me Dr. Reynolds."

His eyes widened in surprise. "She was way out of bounds here."

"*She* was out of bounds?"

Collier cleared his throat. "She can't keep running off half-cocked, putting herself in danger. You were there last time. You saw what happened."

"So, you were what—protecting her? Saving her from herself?" Her throat tightened in anger, her voice cracking. "By handcuffing her and treating her like a criminal. Did you hurt her?"

"What?" Collier looked shocked and confused. "No, I didn't—"

"Did you ask her?" She cut him off. He stared at her mutely, the muscles in his jaw bunching. "You're going to sit here and feed me some bullshit line about protecting her but you didn't even make sure she was okay? Jesus Christ, Jim, she's barely two months out from serious injuries." Thayer raked her hands through her hair, and shook her head. "You're punishing her."

"What?"

"You're punishing her." Thayer nodded slowly as she came to the realization. "Like the parent of a young child who runs into the street after their ball and nearly gets hit. They're just acting on instinct, but that parent watching is so terrified of what might have happened they lash out in anger, scaring them in the hopes they never do it again." She cringed inwardly at comparing Corey to an impulsive child, but she could see her words hit home.

Collier had the decency to look shamefaced. He cleared his throat and covered his emotion by leaning over, opening a drawer. He set Corey's wallet, phone, and glasses on the desk in front of her.

Thayer picked up her glasses, frowning as she glanced around the obnoxiously lit room, fluorescent lights humming and flickering. She stood and snatched up Corey's things, jamming them into her purse. "Take me to her—now."

CHAPTER TWENTY-TWO

They took the stairs to the basement. The floor was cement and the walls yellow painted cinderblock. It was cold and harsh. The lights were bright and unforgiving, making everyone she passed a sickly color.

There was a bench bolted to the floor with a man cuffed to it by one wrist. He was slumped over, head on his chest, and Thayer had to stop herself from reaching out to take his pulse. He smelled like vomit, booze, and urine, but she could see the steady rise and fall of his chest.

Jim led them through a swinging door and into a small room with an officer behind a desk, a camera set up in one corner against a white wall with black hash marks along one side marking heights.

"Sarge." The officer nodded. "What can I do for you?"

"I need someone out of holding. The woman I brought in an hour ago."

The officer nodded. "The drunk?"

Thayer shook her head sharply. "She wasn't drunk."

"Corey Curtis," Collier specified.

"Yeah, I know." The officer nodded and tapped on his keyboard. "The tall one. She started puking all over the place twenty minutes after you left. Then she passed out in the cell. Maintenance just left a few minutes ago after cleaning it up."

Thayer's heart lodged in her throat, her voice panicked. "Get me in there, now."

"Buzz us in." Collier grasped the handle of the heavy steel door. "Open her cell."

She could hear male voices to the left, echoing around a cavernous space, but he guided her down a hallway to the right. She heard the loud echoing clank of metal as a cell door was released and she rounded a corner opening into the holding area.

Thayer's breath caught, tears springing to her eyes at Corey huddled on her side on a narrow bench facing the wall. Her arms were wrapped tightly around herself. The lights were harsh and the cell smelled musty.

"Corey, I'm here." She knelt next to her and placed a hand against her cheek. Her skin was pale and clammy and her breathing shallow, her eyes tightly closed.

Thayer whipped off the sweatshirt she still wore and covered her, but Corey didn't give any indication she was aware. She rummaged in her purse for her medication and the bottle of water, wanting to be prepared, but desperately hoping she wouldn't need it. She turned Corey's head and pressed the meds past her lips, angling the water to her mouth, getting it into her.

"What's wrong with her?" Collier asked. "Do you want me to call an ambulance?"

"They can't help her." She glared at him. "It's a migraine—a bad one. Effects of the head injury. They're triggered when she's under extreme physical or emotional stress or from exposure to bright, harsh light. What the hell did you think the glasses were for anyway?"

"I didn't know." His eyes were worried. "She never said."

"Help me get her up. We need to get her out of here. Is there somewhere we can take her? Somewhere we can make dark and she'll be comfortable?"

"Yeah." Collier stepped forward. "I got her." He slid his hands beneath her shoulders and behind her knees lifting her in his arms. Corey groaned, cracking her eyes, dull with pain and exhaustion.

"It's all right, sweetheart." Thayer was immensely grateful in that moment for Jim Collier's size and strength as he effortlessly lifted her five-foot-ten-inch frame.

"Sarge?" the officer asked in surprise as they moved hurriedly past him.

"I'll do the release paperwork later," Collier said and led them to an elevator.

Back on the second floor they were fortunate not to run into anyone else as Collier led them down a hallway off the main room and kicked open the door to a dark room. "It's for families or interviews with children."

The room was small but there was a full sofa and chair, table and small refrigerator with microwave and coffeemaker on top. In the corner was a plastic bin, overflowing with worn toys and coloring books.

"Can you get her down on her stomach?" Thayer asked as she adjusted the lights to a level that allowed her to see but wouldn't aggravate Corey.

Collier shifted her in his arms as he lowered her to the sofa and carefully rolled her onto her front, turning her head gently to face out. "What can I do?"

"You've done enough," Thayer said sharply. She perched on the edge of the sofa and raised Corey's T-shirt, before coating her hands in peppermint oil. "Please see we aren't disturbed."

"Sergeant Collier, a word, please," a woman's voice commanded from the hallway.

Thayer stilled her hands against Corey's shoulders and turned at the sharp voice to see Jim slip quickly out of the room and close the door. With little other sound but Corey's irregular breathing, she could hear the exchange well enough. She wished she could close out the voices, not wanting to deal with anyone else's anger or problems tonight.

He began. "Not here."

"Here's fine." The woman went on, likely unaware she was being overheard. "Sergeant, you seriously crossed the line tonight. You could make those garbage charges stick if you really wanted, but you will do it without my help."

"You wanna dial it down a notch, Officer Austin?" Jim growled, and Thayer suspected it was more concern over being overheard than over her hostile rebuke.

"No, sir, I do not. I will accept an official insubordination reprimand in my jacket if that's what you feel is necessary, and if it torpedoes my chance of advancement, so be it. I will not be silent on matters of abuse of power. Arresting Corey the way you did and in front of Thayer and her friends, after the help they have provided this department and everything they've been through wasn't just wrong, it was cruel and I'm ashamed to have been a part of it."

Thayer released a slow breath and resumed her massage. She had assumed from the woman's tone it was a commanding officer but now knew she was listening to Steph Austin vent her rage against Jim. There was a long pause and Thayer tilted her head toward the door, curious now.

"Did you know she gets migraines since her head injury?" Jim asked.

"Not specifically. She hides it pretty well but it's obvious to anyone paying attention she's not completely healed." Steph's voice lowered but lost none of its edge. "Why?"

"She got one after I left her in holding, after I humiliated her on the street, hauled her in and took her glasses that help block out the fluorescent light." He said it loudly enough that Thayer suspected he wanted her to hear him take responsibility. "The booking officer assumed she was drunk. She was throwing up and passed out in the cell."

"Jesus. Is Thayer here?"

"Yeah. She must have expected this might happen and came with some pills for her. She was barely conscious when we got to her. I carried her up here."

"Where?"

"In there."

Thayer heard the door handle turn.

"No," Jim said. "Not right now. Doc Reynolds will take of her."

"I should get back out there," Steph said after a long moment of silence or conversation she couldn't hear. "We still haven't found these assholes."

"No. You're off the clock."

"You're benching me?"

"Go home and get some sleep, Austin. That's an order. You look like hell. I'll see you back here in the morning."

"Yes, sir."

Thayer stood and stretched, feeling her joints pop from the few hours of sleep she got in the chair. She moved back to the sofa and perched next to Corey who was sleeping deeply and comfortably on her side. She brushed hair off her face and kissed her temple.

Thayer had spent nearly an hour massaging her back and neck with oil until she finally felt her muscles loosen. The pain must have been excruciating, and the thought of Corey going through that alone in a jail cell made her want to scream in rage.

Instead she busied herself investigating what the room had to offer. The small fridge held several bottles of water and juice and a couple small cartons of milk. There was a tiny freezer and some popsicles. There was a small cabinet over the microwave that had coffee and filters so she set about making a pot. She could use one and she suspected Corey would need one soon.

There was a soft knock at the door and she heard the unmistakable sound of Jim's voice from the other side. She cracked the door to see him looking as beat as she felt. She moved away from the door to let him in.

"You okay, Doc, er, Dr. Reynolds?" he asked, unable to meet her eyes.

"Forget that, please, Jim," Thayer said. "I'm too tired to be angry right now."

"I'm sorry," he said gruffly. "Everything you said. You were right."

Thayer pressed her lips together seeing the profound remorse etched across his face. "I'm not the one you need to apologize to."

His eyes moved past her to Corey and his breath shuddered with a level of emotion Thayer had never heard from him. "I don't know where to start."

Thayer gave his arm a squeeze. "Just talk to her, Jim." Thayer scooped up her purse. "I'm going to find a washroom."

"Just down the hall on the left." He handed her a visitor's pass to clip on and gestured down the hall.

Thayer paused at the door, unsure if leaving Corey alone with him was the right thing to do. She knew she would wake up disoriented and weak, but she hoped if they talked and Corey didn't hold back, there would be a chance they could salvage their friendship.

CHAPTER TWENTY-THREE

Corey's head felt foggy and her mouth felt like it was stuffed with cotton as she struggled to open her eyes. She was crashed out on something soft but she didn't recognize it as either her bed or Thayer's. She smelled coffee close by, much too close unless she was sleeping in the kitchen.

She groaned and dragged her eyes open. It was dim and she had no memory of how she got here or where here was. She pushed herself up on shaky arms.

"Go slow," a deep voice rumbled and she looked around, her head spinning with the movement. Her gaze finally found Collier, a mug of coffee in his hand. She sat up on the sofa, dropping her head into her hands. Her world was spinning in what she recognized as a post migraine fog of confusion and medication.

"Are you all right?"

She raised her head, unsure how to answer as the memories of last night and what he put her through came rushing back, up until the point they arrived at the station. After that she had no memory of what had happened. She saw her phone, wallet, and glasses on the small table in front of her. "I need to call Thayer." Her voice was rough and her hand shaky as she reached for the phone.

"She's here. Been here all night. She just went to the washroom."

Corey nodded and dropped back against the sofa closing her eyes. "Am I still under arrest?"

"No. I dropped all the charges. It's like it never happened."

"Like it never happened. Yeah, just like that."

He poured another mug of coffee and set it on the table in front of her. "I meant there will be no record of your arrest."

"I know what you meant." She eyed the coffee from beneath her lashes. "I need some water first. Is there water?"

He produced a bottle and opened it for her before setting it down and taking the chair across from her.

She was shaking so badly that she had to hold the bottle with two hands to keep from spilling it all over herself. It must have been a bad one. "Where are we?" she asked after draining half of it.

"At the station. In one of the family interview rooms."

"How did I get here?"

He looked away from her, his jaw clenching. "I carried you."

She breathed a humorless laugh. "That must have really fluffed your fucking ego, huh?"

His eyes snapped back to her. "Why didn't you tell me about your migraines?"

"When was I going to do that? Before or after you arrested me?"

"If I had known I wouldn't have—"

"You wouldn't have what? Put your hands on me in anger? Pushed me around? Fucking handcuffed me? I bet you fucking loved that."

He swallowed audibly and cleared his throat. "I'm not going to insult you by asking for your forgiveness for what I did to you, but I hope you will, at least, hear my apology."

She took several deep breaths to try and calm down, or she'd roll right into another migraine. She tried to pick up the coffee but she couldn't hold the mug, even in two hands, without sloshing it everywhere.

He plucked it deftly from her hands and poured a third of it into his own mug before handing it back to her. She eyed him curiously, as he seemed so lost in thought about what he was about to say that he didn't even notice his act of kindness. "I'm listening." Corey sat back, cradling the more manageable mug to her chest.

"I know we like to pretend we don't care about each other. I think you know that's not true—at least for me. You may feel differently, especially after last night." He looked up, seemingly expecting some kind of comment.

Corey offered a small shrug, too tired and angry to help him out.

"I think you are…remarkable. And I'm proud to call you my friend."

Corey's brows rose at him in surprise.

"I also think you are pigheaded and reckless and when I learned you ran after those punks like some lunatic, putting yourself in the line of fire like at the construction site…"

She didn't have the reserves to guess what he was trying to say so she stayed silent, watching him and trying to get a handle on her own ragged emotions.

"I understand your anger and your instinct to protect those you love. Hell, I share it and that's why when I heard you were in danger again, I didn't even have to imagine what that looks and feels like because I already know and I just…" He cleared his throat several times. "The world is a better place with you in it. Jesus, I don't know what I was thinking."

Her brain was so fried she was having a hard time picking apart words so uncharacteristic of him, but if she didn't know better, he just told her he loved her, but she couldn't hear it yet. "You used your power to hurt me." She could barely speak around the emotion clogging her throat and the intense feeling of betrayal. "You wouldn't talk to me or even look at me the whole way here, and then you just left me alone in a fucking jail cell."

His head hung. "Christ, Corey, I—"

"Don't you dare fucking call me that," she snarled, knowing he only ever used her first name to express affection for her like a term of endearment. She couldn't handle it. Not from him. Not now. Her trembling hands were too much even for half a mug of coffee and she set it on the table with a clatter and splash of liquid. "What do you want from me?"

He looked up at her again. "A chance to set things right with you. To earn your trust back."

Like every day after a migraine that needed medication, her emotions were exposed and fragile, and Collier arresting her one moment and begging her forgiveness the next was too much. Her humiliation was complete when she started to cry silently. She swiped furiously at the hot tears streaming down her face. She was enraged at her weakness in front of him, and couldn't bear the sympathy and regret in his eyes.

"I'll find Doc." His voice was hoarse with emotion.

"I'm here." The door opened immediately letting them both know Thayer had been just outside the door.

Corey saw Thayer and the love and tenderness in her golden eyes and came completely undone as Thayer crossed the room to sit next to her, wrapping her in a strong embrace, stroking her back and whispering soothing words. They never heard the door close as Collier left.

After a few minutes Corey took a shuddering breath and pulled away. "I need to speak with Collier again."

Thayer shook her head. "I think you two could use some time away from each other."

"It's not about me," Corey insisted.

Thayer thumbed away the last of her tears. "You're exhausted, sweetheart. It can wait."

"No, it can't wait. I saw them. I remember and I need to give him a description and…Rachel?"

Thayer smiled gently. "She's okay. A few sutures. Maybe a badass scar on her arm. Dana left me a message this morning. Rachel is already back to work supervising the cleanup and repairs."

Corey breathed in relief. "That sounds about right."

"No one else went to the hospital. Some people were pretty shaken up but otherwise fine. The girls saw what happened to you, though, and are worried. I've already texted to say you're all right and not in any trouble. I kind of got the impression Rachel was disappointed she wasn't going to get to visit you in prison."

Corey laughed and it felt really good. She already knew she would forgive Collier. Like him she was no stranger to mishandling her emotions. But not today and probably not tomorrow. She was too raw. "I need to talk to him before the memory fades."

Thayer reached for Corey's glasses. "Put these on. It's worse than the hospital out there."

She blinked and squinted as her eyes struggled to adjust to the harsh light and was assaulted by the cacophony of voices, telephones ringing, and clacking of fingers on keyboards. She swayed slightly, feeling weak, but steadied when Thayer's arm went around her waist. "Holy shit." She breathed as she looked around at the men and women busy protecting and serving. "It's like a fucking dog pound in here."

"Come on."

They wended their way to the far side of the room, both of them doing their best to ignore the glances from around the room.

As they approached the desk, Corey saw Collier and Steph sitting together and a tall stately African-American woman in a crisp white uniform top and sharply creased black slacks hovering over their shoulders looking intently at his monitor.

"I want to give my statement," Corey said to announce their presence and met each of their eyes in turn, working hard to keep her voice steady.

The woman straightened and regarded her for a moment. Her hair was cropped close to her head but it made her look anything but unfeminine. She had small diamond studs in each ear that flashed brightly against her dark skin, which was virtually unlined, but something in her dark eyes told Corey she was much older than she looked.

Steph smiled at them, her brows knitted together with concern. Collier pushed himself out of his chair and cleared his throat. "Corey Curtis, Dr. Thayer Reynolds this is Lieutenant Charlene Williams, head of Narcotics."

Thayer extended her hand. "It's nice to meet you, Lieutenant Williams."

"And you, Dr. Reynolds." She shook her hand.

"Is that the division you work for?" Thayer asked Collier. "Narcotics?"

Lieutenant Williams replied, "Sergeant Collier is the IOL, the cumbersomely named, Interdivisional Operations Liaison. Or, the title I'm not supposed to know— Shit-holder."

Thayer shrugged. "I'm sorry, I don't know what any of that means."

"All the divisions have their own detectives and sergeants above them and lieutenants and captains and on and on up the chain. It's an experimental position to have someone experienced in multiple divisions who can liaise when cases overlap or pick up cases that don't really fall neatly into a division. That's Collier."

"Noted," Corey muttered.

"Ms. Curtis." Lieutenant Williams held out her hand and waited for Corey to shake it before continuing. "Sergeant Collier has informed his superiors of his arguably lawful, but most certainly inappropriate, arrest of you last night and your subsequent illness while in holding—full disclosure. If you would like to file a complaint regarding your treatment by an officer of this department, please know we will take it very seriously."

Corey sucked in a sharp breath and couldn't help notice Steph do the same. Her gaze was steady on Collier whose face was unreadable. "No, ma'am, I do not. Collier and I have always managed to resolve our differences. This time will be more challenging but I expect that to continue to be true—in time." Her eyes never left him and she saw him release a slow breath. His face was still expressionless but his eyes softened with emotion.

"Very well." Lieutenant Williams seemed satisfied. "I know you've had a difficult night, but if you say you're up for it, I'm sure Collier and Austin would be pleased to take your statement. We could certainly use a break on this." She nodded sharply and left.

Collier gestured to the chair next to his desk and Corey slumped into it, what little energy she had waning.

He dropped into his own chair and looked her over. "You don't have to do this now."

"Yes, I do," she stated firmly. "I want to help if I can."

She felt Thayer's hand warm on the back of her neck. "I'm going to go get you something to eat."

Corey offered her a smile. "Thank you."

Steph jumped up and slid her chair around next to Corey. "You sit," she said to Thayer. "I'll go."

Corey shook her head. "Steph, you don't have to—"

"Quiet." Steph squeezed her shoulder gently. "I get a first responders discount."

Corey turned back to Collier to see him looking at her with concern and bristled. "Stop fucking looking at me like you've broken me," she snapped. "I get headaches still, so what? It could have happened anyway. Last night was fucked up even before you came along. I'm fine."

"Listen, Curtis, I appreciate—"

"If you're going to talk about anything other than this case, I cannot hear you right now." Corey swallowed hard. "Just get your damn notebook out."

He nodded and pulled out his notebook. "Go ahead."

"There were six of them."

"Six?" He looked up. "You're sure?"

"Yes." Corey nodded slowly. "I couldn't tell right away. When I was running after them they were moving really erratically, weaving back and forth, but when we got to the fence there were three already on the other side, two dropping down and one sitting on top."

"Could you tell how old they are?"

"If any of them is over twenty-five I'd be shocked."

"But not kids?"

"No." She shook her head. "Older than that for sure but not very big. I don't think a single one was taller than I am. They all looked slight, wiry like they haven't filled out yet or don't eat enough."

"White?"

"Yes, all of them."

"What else?"

"I'd guess they were all on something. The way they laughed and moved seemed unnatural and they talked really fast."

"And you got a good look at one of them? Austin saw him on top of the fence, but didn't get a good look at his face."

"Yeah. White, early twenties, slight build, brown eyes, thin, long brown hair. He looked unwashed, greasy with a bad complexion and sharp features."

"That all fits."

"With what?"

"Sounds like the group we've been looking for. The vandalism and burglaries. Some reports say 'pack of kids,' some 'wild boys,' some 'thugs' and we've never had a description until now. They've stayed away from directly assaulting people and populated or occupied buildings until last night."

"You think this is related to your drug ring? To the body at the lake?"

"I do. I'm just not sure how yet. At the very least, they're using and getting a line on them could lead us to the rest." He tapped his pen on his desk. "You okay to go through some photos? See if you recognize one of them?"

"Yeah, I'm good.

CHAPTER TWENTY-FOUR

"Fuck. He's not fucking here." She raked her hands through her hair. It was well after noon when Corey slammed the last book closed.

Steph and Thayer had been out again for food and coffee and Corey's hand tremor now was more than likely the result of all the caffeine she had consumed to battle back the sedatives and total exhaustion.

"It's fine, Curtis." Collier stacked the photo books on his desk. "We have your description. It's good."

She knew he was just as frustrated but had been holding back. All their normal easy banter and good-natured ribbing was gone. He had been tense and careful with her, checking his words on more than one occasion, and every time it reminded Corey of why he felt he needed to, adding weight to her already heavy heart. She didn't want them to be so damaged, and though they never socialized or saw each other except over a dead body, she felt the loss of their friendship acutely.

"We'll put out your description. Something will turn up." He looked at her and she couldn't stand the look of regret on his face, but she didn't have the words to ease his pain.

Thayer slid her hand around her shoulder. "It's time to go, sweetheart."

She turned and looked at her for the first time in hours, seeing her own fatigue mirrored in Thayer's face. "Yeah."

"I'll walk you out." Steph stood from where she'd perched on the edge of her desk.

Corey gestured to the stack of books. "Sorry, I wasn't more help."

Collier met her gaze. He opened his mouth to speak and slammed it shut. Corey had no idea what he was going to say and her heart cracked open again at their distance. "You helped," he finally commented. "You always help."

The sun was clouded over but the afternoon warm as they made their way to the visitor lot, giving Corey some needed respite from the brutal lighting of the precinct. Thayer unlocked the passenger side of Corey's truck and waited for her to settle.

Steph sighed, lips pressed in a hard line as she looked at them. "We'll find him." She placed a hand on Corey's arm through the open window. "Are you okay?"

Corey simply nodded.

"I'm sorry about what happened last night."

Thayer bristled. "Don't apologize for him."

"I'm not," Steph replied and met their eyes in turn. "I told you my job was to protect you." She looked at Corey. "And I didn't do that."

Corey raised her head, shaking it slowly. "It's okay. It wasn't your fault," she rasped, her awareness fading. "Have you found Harold Crandall?"

"No."

"Is there a warrant out for his arrest?" Thayer asked.

"For what?" Steph gestured helplessly. "We can't connect him to anything. Right now he's just wanted for questioning with regard to the body of his nephew found on the property that he's actually not the legal owner of. We have shit. But the longer he stays hidden, the more convinced I am he's good for something, though it's not looking like murder. No activity on his cards or accounts. No trace on his cell number. No sign of his car. Mail hasn't been picked up. He's definitely lying low and using cash. No sign of that damn boat that everyone knows but no one has seen. I mean, Jesus, we're not talking Lake Superior. It's like a little over two square miles and drains to the river via a couple of small creeks, which may or not be large enough to get a boat down depending on the time of year. I just don't understand."

Thayer shrugged. "There are a lot of inlets and islands. It would be pretty easy to tuck away for a while and stay hidden."

"I don't think he's staying hidden exactly. I think he's still operating. I just don't know how."

"You positively identified the body as Robert Crandall?" Corey mumbled into her arm.

"You didn't hear that from me."

Corey raised her head. "I don't care right now."

Steph offered them a small smile. "I have to go. Get some rest, you two."

"Corey, honey." Thayer caressed her face to wake her, her eyes fluttering open. "We're home." Thayer had wanted to drive straight back but knew she had to get errands out of the way first or she'd fall into to bed and never go back out.

Corey had fallen asleep within minutes of leaving the station and showed no sign of stirring each time Thayer stopped, so she left her in the truck and took care of the shopping and drug store after noticing Corey's prescriptions needed to be refilled.

Corey swallowed and nodded. "'kay." She stumbled out of the truck toward the house. "I need a shower."

Thayer unlocked the door and waited to make sure her shower was under way before bringing in the groceries. She powered through and made a large pan of lasagna as well. She knew Corey loved it and they could eat it all weekend. It was in the oven on low while Thayer took her own shower and crawled into bed, snuggling close to Corey's warm, naked body, breathing in the smell of her freshly washed hair and soft, clean skin.

Thayer was on the deck, eyes closed, basking in the warmth of the last of the late afternoon sun after her nap. The slider opened and she turned and smiled. Corey padded out in bare feet, faded, low-slung jeans and T-shirt. Her hair was sticking up carelessly, her yellow-tinted glasses not enough to hide her bright eyes but changing their color to blue-green.

Thayer felt herself fall in love all over again at Corey's sleepy smile and casual slouch, the way her shirt pulled up, revealing a flash of tight abs, as she drank from the bottle of beer between her fingers.

Thayer arched a brow in silent admonishment.

"Don't worry." Corey smiled crookedly, obviously pretending to misunderstand the look. "I brought you one too." She set another beer on the arm of Thayer's chair.

She couldn't help her smile as Corey settled into the chair next to her and tipped her beer toward her. They clinked bottles and sat back, the silence comfortable and safe. A heron flew low across the lake and a mallard pair paddled lazily, fishing for dinner just off her dock against the soundtrack of birdsong and breeze against the trees, the tops of a few just starting to show a hint of fall color.

"Do you want to talk about it?" Thayer asked quietly.

Corey took a long drink of her beer. "My heart hurts. I'm afraid we're broken."

Thayer could hear the sadness in her voice. "Irreparably?"

"I don't know how he and I can ever be the same after this."

"It doesn't have to be the same to be fixed, does it? Like the Japanese art of Kintsugi when broken pottery is repaired with gold or platinum. A break becomes an honored part of its story instead of trying to cover it up like it didn't happen."

Corey smiled. "You should have been a philosopher."

Thayer let the beauty of the lake wash over them again as the sun moved lower in the sky. "We were broken once not that long ago," she said softly. "Now we're whole again but not the same. We're stronger. We're better."

"Yes, I've been thinking about that too."

"Tell me," Thayer encouraged.

"The other day when Collier and I were getting in each other's face and you said we were a lot alike... Steph said the same thing to me later that morning and even Rachel had something to say about it last night." Corey leaned forward in her chair swinging her bottle between her fingers. "I guess I see it a lot better now. It's not exactly the same, but when I got injured and I got scared, I was way out of my depth emotionally. I was seriously incapable of dealing with my own shit. I lashed out at you because, like Collier, when things get heavy my default emotion is anger."

Thayer's eyes sparkled. "That's very insightful and self-aware, sweetheart."

"I know, right?"

"So what do you want to do?" She grew serious, her own anger simmering again. "What he did to you, for many it would be an unforgivable abuse."

Corey winced. "Is it for you?"

It was Thayer's turn to sigh heavily. "That's not my decision to make."

"I want to know what you think, Thayer."

"I think Jim Collier loves you more than he will ever let on. I think no one feels worse about what happened than he does. I think that even your forgiveness won't alleviate the guilt he feels about hurting you. He will be hardest on himself, just like you were."

"Yeah. I think so too."

"If it helps, last night I overheard Steph giving him hell over what happened. It was bloody."

"Really?" Corey's mouth gaped. "Good for her. She's perfect for him."

"Uh-huh. What are you going to do?"

"I knew the answer to that the moment I woke up this morning," she admitted. "But I don't want to think about it anymore tonight."

"I love you very much, Corey Curtis." Thayer reached for her hand, lacing their fingers together. "Would you like to eat out here? I made lasagna."

"I know." Corey's eyes flashed mischievously. "It's your best one yet."

Thayer scowled playfully. "Cheater."

CHAPTER TWENTY-FIVE

Corey was having the loveliest time on a picnic with Thayer and Michelle Obama until "The Imperial March" from *Star Wars* started playing, interrupting them, and some kid kept tugging at her arm, asking if she got her tattoo in prison.

"Corey." Thayer shook her arm, her voice gravelly with sleep. "Corey, your phone."

"What?"

"Answer your phone," Thayer mumbled before rolling over and putting a pillow over her head.

The ringtone stopped and Corey sighed. Letting her eyes close again for a moment when the music started again. She heard Thayer groan from beneath the pillow.

Corey banged her hand around on the nightstand to find her phone. "'lo?"

"Curtis, it's Collier."

"Yeah, I know." Corey rubbed her tired eyes. "What the hell time is it?"

"Late. Or early."

Corey held her phone away from her face for a second and squinted at the display. "Why the hell are you calling me at three seventeen in the morning?"

"I'm, uh, sorry to bother you but I need you to come down to the hospital."

Corey paused, absorbing his words before shooting bolt upright. "Jesus, what's wrong? Are you all right?"

"What? Yes. I'm fine. Everyone is fine. I didn't mean to alarm you."

"Corey?" Thayer's sleepy voice questioned in concern and she reached for Corey.

"It's okay, babe," Corey said. "What's going on?"

"There was an OD last night. He fits the description of your guy. Can you come take a look at him?"

"Yeah," Corey said. "The morgue?"

"He's still in the ED."

"Give me half an hour."

Thayer flicked on the light. "Is everything all right?"

She scrubbed her face. "Collier thinks they might have one of the guys that trashed Rachel's place. Died in the ED tonight, er, this morning. He wants me to come down."

"Okay. I'll get dressed."

Corey grabbed her before she had a chance to get out of bed and pulled her back, wrapping an arm around her naked waist. "I would rather you didn't." She brushed an unruly lock of hair from Thayer's face and nuzzled her neck. "I like you like this."

Thayer dropped her head back. "You shouldn't go alone."

"I need you here…" Corey kissed her neck and along her jaw, ending at her lips. "…keeping the bed warm and giving me something to look forward to coming home to. You know, after leftover lasagna."

Thayer laughed and smooshed Corey's face between her hands, kissing her hard. "What would happen if I were lying naked in bed with a plate of lasagna on my chest?"

Corey's face screwed up in thought. "Is the lasagna hot?"

Collier was waiting for her at the entrance to the ED. "Thanks for coming."

"Yeah, sure. I wasn't doing anything else."

He stopped and stared at her, looking like he wanted to say something.

"It was a joke," Corey added. "I was sleeping." She slipped her glasses off the collar of her shirt and put them on as they headed through the sliding doors. "How did you find him?"

"A patrol car responded to a call from a twenty-four-hour corner store downtown. A group of kids loitering, smashing bottles and trying to flip a dumpster. By the time they arrived there was just the one in some sort of psychotic episode in the parking lot and the others had taken off. We had your description out and I got the call."

Sunday at four o'clock in the morning wasn't a popular time to be out and about, wrecking yourself. The ED was nearly empty. Corey nodded to a few familiar faces as she followed Collier into curtain four. Jules was packing up the monitors and unhooking the IV from the port of the sheet-wrapped body.

"Corey?" She dropped what she was doing to give Corey a hug. "What are you doing here? Are you all right? We were really worried about you."

"Hey, Jules." Corey returned her embrace. "Yeah, thanks, I'm good. I'm just consulting with the police on something." She gestured to Collier. "You know Jim Collier?"

"Sure, I've seen you around." Her eyes narrowed. "You arrested Corey Friday night. Why?"

Collier swallowed. "Uh, it was—"

"A misunderstanding. So, you have the graveyard shift, huh? No pun intended. "Yeah." Jules rolled her eyes.

"Do you know anything about this patient?" Collier asked.

"Besides the obvious? No. I just need some of the equipment from in here. I can get the doctor that pronounced him if you want."

"Thanks." Collier pulled out his notebook.

"I'll send him down." Jules wheeled the heart rate monitor out the door. "See ya, Corey."

Corey leaned against the counter and jammed her hands in her pockets while Collier kept his head bent, scribbling away in his notebook. The weight of the elephant in the room was oppressive. "So, I guess I know what I'm doing Monday," she commented to break the silence.

Collier grunted but didn't look up. "I paged Webster. I want the post done tomorrow—or today—whatever."

"Shit." Corey groaned. "Sunday?"

"You're not doing it. The resident is."

Corey sucked a breath through her teeth. "Don't do that."

"Do what?"

"Treat me like I'm made of glass."

"I'm not. I didn't. It was Webster's idea."

Corey's jaw clenched and unclenched in anger.

Collier closed his notebook. "You were pretty ragged yesterday morning."

"Yeah, your brain on fire and a gut full of sedatives tends to fuck you up for a while." She seethed. "So, you got to see me lose it. Yay, you."

"I'm sor—"

"Stop fucking apologizing to me." She raked her hands through her hair and took a breath. "That wasn't my first migraine, and believe it or not, it wasn't the first time I've been arrested."

"Oh, I believe it."

Corey couldn't help the laugh that burst out of her. Her expression turned stony the next instant and she straightened from the counter when Watson Gregory stepped through the curtain.

"Whoa." Collier's eyes went wide at her alert. "What?"

Dr. Gregory froze when he saw Corey, his lip curling. "What, you like 'em still warm?"

Collier stepped between the two of them pointing to the badge clipped to his belt. "She's with me."

His eyes darted to Collier's badge and back to Corey, baring his teeth. "I assume she's under arrest for assault."

Corey couldn't help a snort of laughter at the irony.

Collier took a step toward him, backing him up. Dr. Gregory was tall but Collier topped him by two inches and at least fifty pounds. "The way I hear it you're the one who should be concerned about assault charges."

Dr. Gregory paled, his eyes going to Corey for a moment. She offered him a small shrug.

He cleared his throat nervously. "What can I help you with, Officer?"

"Sergeant. We want to look at the deceased."

"Of course, Sergeant." Dr. Gregory moved to the shrouded body and carefully unwrapped the sheet from his head, pulling it down to the chest before stepping back.

Corey's eyes moved to the body and she sucked in a breath at the waxy skin, eyes partially closed and clouded in death. "It's him."

"What was the cause of death?" Collier asked.

Dr. Gregory relaxed somewhat. "Presented with extreme hypertension, tachycardia, fever, and altered mental status. When we could understand him, he complained of chest and stomach pain and he crashed within twenty minutes." His gaze darted to Corey and he shrugged. "Autopsy will probably show stroke or MI. Or both."

"Drug overdose?" Collier asked.

"Without a doubt."

"Crystal meth?"

"Sure, yeah." He nodded. "That works."

"Did he say anything before he died?"

"Very little that was intelligible and even less that was coherent."

Collier nodded. "I'll need his clothes and all personal effects."

"Sure." Watson Gregory pulled the sheet down farther and plucked a large sealed biohazard bag from between the body's legs and passed it over. "Anything else?"

"No." Collier was already moving to the counter with the bag and didn't look up. "Thank you for your time."

Corey joined Collier at the counter while Watson Gregory disappeared without another word.

Collier flipped open the tatty Velcro wallet and removed the vic's driver's license. "Andrew Arthur Weeks, twenty-three years old." He paused and pulled out a worn punch card with several holes around the outside. "Gotcha."

"What's that?" Corey asked and he held it up. "Where's Jake's Bait and Tackle? And what the hell is a Green Machine trolling lure?"

"Jake's is farther around the lake at the west end of Old South Road, and Green Machine is a lure for deep sea fishing—tuna and marlin."

"Why would a bait shop at Rankins Lake be selling it?"

"They wouldn't."

"You think that has something to do with the drugs?"

"Yup."

"So, what now?"

"Now I go break the tragic news to Andrew Weeks's family and find out who his friends are and pick them up."

"His five friends. Do you have enough to arrest them?"

"Not yet, but they don't know that and for all those shit for brains know, Weeks is still alive and gave them up to get back at them for leaving him to the cops." His mouth quirked wickedly. "Guaranteed at least one of those losers has a record and one of them is too stupid to keep his mouth shut and lawyer up."

"Cool." Corey suddenly felt incredibly tired as she took off her glasses, and forgetting about her broken nose, scrubbed her face. "Ah, shit." She winced.

"You okay?"

"I'm fine." She held up a hand and slipped her glasses back on. "I should go, unless you need something else?"

"No." He gathered up Andrew Weeks's things. "Let's get out of here."

They walked out together toward her truck.

"Thanks again for coming down," he said.

"Yeah." Corey breathed wearily.

"Are we ever going to be okay?" he asked after a long moment.

Corey turned and leaned against her truck, hands in her pockets. "You want to make it up to me, Collier? Be there for me when it counts."

CHAPTER TWENTY-SIX

"Aw, babe, what are you doing up?" Corey asked as she dropped her keys and glasses on the counter and saw Thayer wrapped in her robe huddled over a mug of tea.

Thayer smiled, relieved. "I was worried."

Corey draped her arms over Thayer's shoulders, kissing her neck. "It hasn't been that long."

Thayer hugged Corey's waist, pressing her face into her belly. "The bed was cold."

"Yeah," Corey agreed tiredly and dropped into a chair. She gestured to the mug. "Is there more?"

"I'll get it." Thayer rose and moved to the kitchen. "Chamomile okay? It'll help you sleep."

Corey rested her head on her arms. "Not sure I'm going to need any help in that department."

"How did it go?" Thayer set a steaming mug in front of her.

Corey wrapped her hands around it and stuck her face into the steam. "It was him."

Thayer nodded. "And with Jim?"

"Oh, he's on the hunt now to end this case with some shifty cop tricks." Corey smiled. "I'm sure it will all be solved by later today."

"I meant with you and Jim."

"Oh, right." Corey sipped her tea. "We're on the road to recovery, I think."

Thayer reached across the table and gripped her hand. "I'm really happy about that."

"Me too."

"We have a brunch date with Nana."

"Since when?"

"Since twenty minutes ago."

Corey checked her watch. It was just creeping toward six. "You called her at five thirty?"

"She called me," Thayer replied grimly. "I think she's ready to give me my verbal switching over what happened with you."

Corey grimaced. "Sorry, babe."

"She said she put in a special request with the kitchen for us."

"Meaning?"

"Meaning steak and eggs for you probably and arsenic-laced cookies for me."

Corey laughed. "Come on, Thayer. Lil thinks you shit ice cream."

Thayer snorted. "Well, that's hot."

"Sorry." Corey grinned. "My filter is still on the fritz." She rubbed her eyes. "Wait, you can do that there? Just request brunch?"

"She can. Nana's like—what's it called on that Australian prison show?"

"Top dog."

"Yes, that's her."

"Good to know. What time are we expected?"

"Ten thirty."

Corey nodded and did some mental math. "So, we have like three hours." She reached for Thayer's hand.

Thayer grinned and pulled her to her feet. "Four," she corrected as she led Corey down the hall. "Three and a half if you want a shower."

"Hey, where's my lasagna?"

"You'll spoil your brunch. I've got the next best thing." Thayer smirked and kicked the bedroom door shut for effect.

"That's weird," Corey commented as they stood around the front of the Pond House for a minute, expecting Lil to come out and greet them. She was always watching for her visitors. "Wonder what she's up to."

"Hmm." Thayer crossed her arms. "Probably sharpening her knives."

"Will you stop," Corey chided lightly and reached for her hand. "You are not in trouble with her. Your grandmother is kind and gracious and generous—just like you."

"We'll soon see," Thayer said, threading her fingers through Corey's. "Let's go around back. She's probably already on the patio."

She was and Corey wasn't immediately on guard when she first saw Lil sitting at the same table that she was at the other day, relaxed and staring out over the pond in quiet contemplation. She didn't hear them approach.

"Good morning, Nana," Thayer greeted her softly.

Lil's head turned to regard Thayer shrewdly for a long moment before she rose and pulled Thayer into a strong one-armed embrace. "Jo."

Something was up. Corey could feel it in the air now, and Thayer was definitely on edge. Lil looked Corey over from head to toe and then back again before pulling her in close with a satisfied twitch of her lips.

Corey met Thayer's eyes over the top of Lil's head but she could only offer a puzzled look.

They sat together, Thayer and Corey on one side and Lil on the other, and Corey busied herself draining her water to avoid having to speak right away.

"So, girls," Lil began, lacing her fingers together and cradling her chin on her hands. "Tell me what you've been up to this weekend."

Corey's throat seized and she coughed to get her last swallow down. She risked a glance to Thayer, who had steepled her hands in front of her face and closed her eyes.

It hadn't even occurred to Corey to worry about who was going to find out about the events of Friday night. Most of her friends were there. Thayer, clearly, hadn't seen this coming either and was quiet as she pressed her lips together in a tight line. Corey could see the wheels spinning as she considered her answer.

"All right, Jo," Lil began. "How about I tell you about my weekend? It was entirely uneventful until last night just after eleven when Mary Margaret Marshall burst into my room and dragged me out to the common room shouting nonsense about my granddaughter's boyfriend on the news, being arrested Friday night by the handsome police officer I was having lunch with the other day."

"*Boy*friend? What the fu—" Corey blurted and then slammed her mouth shut at the identical withering glances from both Thayer and Lil.

"I admit I didn't give it much thought. She's blind as a bat—until she replayed the spot showing this grainy cell phone video, taken by someone downtown. Imagine my shock…" Lil looked expectantly at each of them. "Now, which one of you is going to tell me what you've gotten yourselves mixed up in this time, and which one of you is going to explain to me why I'm finding out about it from the news—again?"

"Nana, we aren't mixed up in anything."

"Oh, really? Then why was Corey being arrested?"

"It was a mistake," Thayer offered. "There were no charges and Jim Collier has apologized. It was upsetting and Corey had a rough night but she's fine." Thayer gestured to Corey who nodded emphatically. "We're both fine, and honestly it didn't occur to either one of us to mention it because it's over, and we didn't even think it might have been newsworthy."

Lil's eyes narrowed at them both and Corey put on her most honest expression, trying to discern Lil's next line of questioning.

"The news segment was about a band of drug-crazed ruffians terrorizing the city."

Corey snorted a laugh. "They didn't really say that, did they?"

"I paraphrased and embellished." Lil frowned at her. "Tell me this doesn't have anything to do with the sergeant's visit and the body on the Crandall property."

Corey chewed on her lip and eyed Thayer, who shrugged in answer to the silent question. "Collier seems to think so," Corey began. "He believes there may be a drug ring operating in the city and the Crandalls—Harold and maybe Robert—are or were involved. That's really all we know, Lil. I promise."

Lil turned her attention to Thayer. "Anything to add, Jo?"

"No, Nana. That's all there is, truly." She reached across the table for her grandmother's hand and held it in her own. "I'm sorry you had to find out like that. There was…" Her eyes flicked to Corey, "…trouble, but we are not *in* any, and we certainly didn't mean for you to feel like we were keeping something from you."

Lil considered them both and Corey saw the moment she was satisfied, her frown relaxed and her eyes sparkled with humor again. "Well, let's have brunch then."

As if by magic, the server came by with three plates, and Corey had never been as thrilled to find out Thayer was correct, steak and eggs. There were also seasoned potatoes, fruit, and assorted pastries.

Corey checked out Thayer's plate, identical to hers, and noticed her hesitation. Thayer stared intensely at her food for so long Corey actually wondered if she could discern the ingredients. She bit her lip to suppress a laugh as she picked up her own plate and switched it with the one in front of Thayer whose answering smile was a mix of embarrassment and gratitude.

"I don't suppose you're going to tell me what that was about?" Lil said dryly.

"Just a private joke." Corey smiled innocently and started on her food.

Lil walked them back to Corey's truck, her strong arm wrapped around Thayer's waist and Corey holding her weakened right hand. "Hey, Lil, I have a question for you," Corey began hesitantly.

"I may or may not have an answer for you."

Corey took a deep breath, hesitating at stirring the pot on this again but went for it anyway. "What does Harold Crandall look like?"

They were already back at Corey's truck when both Thayer and Lil turned to her with eyes narrowed in suspicion. "Why, my dear, would you need to know that?"

Thayer crossed her arms and arched a brow.

"I don't *need* to know," Corey agreed. "I'm just curious."

"Curiosity killed the cat," Lil replied with a smirk.

"Knowledge is power."

"Knowledge isn't power until it's applied."

"The only source of knowledge is experience." Corey laughed.

"For pity's sake, you two, knock it off." Thayer threw up her hands. "Nana, just tell her already."

Corey and Lil grinned at each other like fools. "Keep in mind, the last time I saw Harold Crandall as close as we are now was twenty-five years ago."

"That's fine." Corey gestured for her to go on. "I just want some idea."

"When I knew him, he was at least six feet with sandy brown hair that he always kept a little longer, shaggy even. He was relatively trim with deep-set eyes and pronounced features.

Strong jaw and sharp nose. He had a shallow chin cleft too. Quite handsome, really."

Corey tried to picture the man she was describing. "Anyone you can compare him to? Like an actor or something?" she asked. Out of the corner of her eyes she could see Thayer frowning at her.

"Hmm. Yes, what's the name of the one in those *Ring* movies?"

"You've seen *The Ring*?" Corey's mouth gaped in shock.

"Oh, my, god." Thayer rolled her eyes.

"The ones with the hobbits and the swords." Lil waved her hand around.

"Oh." Corey grinned. "*Lord of the Rings*?"

"That's right. He was in that. He was a warrior of some kind."

Corey's lips pursed in thought. She had seen them but she wasn't that big a fan of the series.

"Aragorn," Thayer offered, looking entirely annoyed.

"That's right. Very good, Jo. Harold Crandall looks a little like him."

CHAPTER TWENTY-SEVEN

Corey flopped onto the sofa with a beer and flipped through the channels of the large HD television until she found the Jets and Giants pre-season game. "Do we have any other plans today?" she called to Thayer, who had disappeared toward the bedroom.

"I don't."

Corey sucked on her beer and stretched her legs out in front of her. "Good."

"Oh." Thayer commented as she came back into the great room several minutes later. "I was going to exercise, though. I need the television for an hour or two."

Corey glanced up at her and nearly spit out her beer. "Holy shit." She coughed, ogling Thayer dressed in form-fitting, black and emerald green Lycra crop pants and a matching racer back tank. "Are you kidding me, right now?"

Thayer took advantage of Corey's distraction and snatched the remote from her hand to switch the input and stream her favorite Pilates and yoga workouts. "Thank you."

"Wait." Corey stood, still staring. "How have I never seen this?" She swept her hand up and down while Thayer unrolled her yoga mat in front of the television.

"Because I make a point never to do this when you're around. So, be gone with you."

"What do you mean?" Corey feigned hurt. "I can't watch?"

"Absolutely not." Thayer lowered herself onto the mat gracefully without using her hands. "You'll distract me."

"I'll distract *you*?" Corey's mouth gaped as Thayer began a series of stretches, her long, toned muscles moving smoothly beneath her bronze skin.

"If you want to watch the game go back to your condo or to the bar," Thayer suggested. "I'll call you when you can come back." Thayer looked over her shoulder, eyes dancing, as she stretched her arms slowly over her head, arching her back and displaying her breasts. "If you want to come back, that is."

Corey sucked in a breath. "You are a wicked tease, babe."

"Only if I don't put out later." Thayer laughed. "Bye."

Corey sat in her truck at the end of the driveway drumming her fingers on the wheel and considering how to spend the next two hours. Going left would take her back into town and somewhere she could watch the game. Going right would take her farther around the lake and to Jake's Bait and Tackle where she had absolutely no business snooping around.

Five minutes later she stopped for the truck in front of her to make a wide turn into the road and back their boat trailer down the ramp to the water. Her fingers tapped against the wheel, her leg jiggling with an anxiety she couldn't define.

The dirt parking lot of Jake's Bait and Tackle was nearly full with trucks and trailers. The weathered, wood-sided building saw a steady stream of customers coming and going. Some headed toward cars and others toward boats tied up at one of the small docks scattered with gas pumps.

Corey stared at the dusty windows of the shop covered with tatty signs for beer, cigarettes, and groceries, along with advertisements for all manner of fishing equipment, boat accessories, and bait. She figured she could just pop in to take a look around and pick up a six-pack for her troubles with no one the wiser. Five minutes tops.

On cue, Darth Vader's theme rang out from her back pocket, signaling another call from Collier. She ignored it, not interested in any more apologies from him. She'd get back to him in her own time.

It rang again as she hopped up the steps to the front door of the shop, the ring interrupted this time by a text chime. She rolled her eyes and pulled the phone, checking the message.

Answer your fucking phone!

Corey jerked to stop at the top step, her eyes widening as she swiped her phone on. "Hello?"

"Do not go in that store," he barked and Corey froze, her head snapping up. "Do not look around. You are thirty seconds away from fucking up an operation and this entire case."

"Shit." Corey tried to relax and stepped back down toward the parking lot.

"Get your ass over here."

"Where?" Corey replied, trying not to look for him.

"The boat launch."

Corey winced as the line disconnected and walked back through the parking lot. She considered just getting back in her truck and driving back to Thayer's, but her curiosity was overwhelming and Collier sounded really pissed. She should probably address that.

"Get in," Collier commanded from the passenger side window of his unmarked car parked off the side of the road, facing the bait shop. Corey bent to look through his window to see Steph glaring at her and shaking her head.

She opened the back door and slid in, realizing her mistake as soon as her ass hit the hard, black vinyl seat and the door slammed closed. She looked at the two of them through the metal cage between the front and rear seats.

Collier's car was unmarked but still very much a police car, which she became acutely aware of as she groped for the door handle on the inside, only to come up empty. "Oh, shit."

"Curtis." Collier turned around and smiled, menacingly, while Steph returned to her surveillance of the shop. "What are you doing here?"

"Would you believe I was thinking about taking up fishing?" Corey offered hesitantly.

"You are such a colossal pain in my ass. I am starting to feel less badly about cuffing you," he thundered.

"Take it easy." Corey raised her hands in apology. "Don't get all eye twitchy on me. I didn't come here to crash your party. I have no idea what you have going on right now. I just wanted to take a look around."

Collier faced front and resumed watching the building, occasionally through binoculars. "It's like you're trying to give me a fucking stroke."

Corey sighed. "Steph, help me out here?"

"Not this time, sister." Steph shook her head, eyes trained forward.

"Sorry. Jesus," she said. "Will you at least tell me what's going on?"

"Here he comes now." Collier ignored her as a small outboard whined its way toward the dock. Collier passed the binoculars to Steph.

"Who's that? Crandall?" Corey straightened and peered through the windshield. She didn't need binoculars to see the lone occupant was a muscular younger man, ratty jeans, T-shirt and stained gray hoodie with a filthy orange cap pulled low over his eyes. "That's not him."

"He looks good," Steph commented as they watched the disheveled and twitchy man make a show of admiring some of the nicer boats before shuffling along the dock to the store.

"Who?" Corey asked, squinting at the man. "Tell me."

"Shut it, Curtis," Collier snapped.

"Fine," Corey huffed. She chewed her lip and started singing an old camp song in a terrible voice. "I don't wanna get married, I'm having too much fun. I don't wanna get married to any certain one."

"Quiet," Collier barked, turning around.

Corey stared pointedly at him. "I've got a lotta girlfriends—I changed that part there—I treat them all the same. To marry one and cheat the rest would be a dirty shame."

"Corey, come on," Steph said, shaking her head.

"Let me out or tell me. I know you've seen *Ghost*. Second verse, same as the first, but a little bit louder and a little bit worse. I don't wanna get married. I'm having too much fun. I don't wanna get married—"

"Christ on the cross," Collier blurted. "It's Officer Warren. He's making a buy. The kids gave up Jake Butler dealing out of the shop. The punch card gets you access. If we can bust Jake, we can get him to roll over on Harold Crandall and make the case, shutting down his distribution network."

"Nicely done." Corey nodded, impressed.

Her compliment seemed to mollify him, his expression softening. "Yeah."

"He's coming out," Steph said.

Collier turned back to look out front. "He give the sign?"

"There it is—cap off, hands through hair, cap back on."

Corey craned to see Kelly Warren make his way back down toward the dock.

"Let's go," Collier said. "I'll call for the warrant. Roll the cars, silent."

Corey sat forward, unable to contain her excitement. She was up close and personal at what was about to be a major drug bust.

Steph moved the car into the lot and parked close to Corey's truck. Her view of the store from the backseat was almost entirely obstructed. Steph and Collier were fully involved with each other and the case as radios crackled and other cars pulled in behind them.

"Hey," Corey barked at them as they got out of the front, paying her no mind at all.

Collier rapped on the glass with his knuckles as he walked by. "Stay put, Curtis."

"Motherfucker." She scrabbled at the door she couldn't open and then rattled the cage between front and back. She wasn't going anywhere and she couldn't watch. At least Steph and Collier had the foresight to leave the front windows down for her. Corey groaned to no one. "Thayer's going to kill me."

CHAPTER TWENTY-EIGHT

Corey tried not to look at her watch every thirty seconds while she listened to the sounds of doors slamming, radios crackling and Collier booming orders. Cars around her fired up as wide-eyed shop patrons left in a cloud of dust, having been cleared of any wrongdoing. She heard the whine and rumble of boat engines start and roar off at speed. The minutes kept ticking by.

An eternity later Steph and Collier reconvened near the car and she could hear snippets of their conversation. Crandall had been identified there by several other patrons. He had come by boat and was intending to get gas until he joined a few men discussing the death of Drew Weeks and the arrest of his buddies. It was reported Crandall got really jumpy and took off again before gassing up.

"He's running," Steph stated.

"At least he won't get very far without gas," Collier replied.

"Unless he gets it somewhere else."

"Get someone contacting the lake residents."

Corey sat up, an uneasy feeling in her gut, and pulled out her phone.

"Hi, sweetheart, I was just going to call you," Thayer answered.

"Are you okay?" Corey asked.

"Of course. Is something wrong?"

Corey exhaled quietly in relief. "Nope. Just checking."

"How's the game?"

"Uh, I'm not watching the game." Corey winced.

"No? Where did you go?"

"Just took a drive around the lake."

"For two hours?"

"Yeah, um…" Corey grimaced. "…I've been held up."

"Corey?"

"Well, um, maybe detained is a better word."

"Tell me."

Corey's words tumbled out on a breath. "I went to Jake's Bait place just to check it out and Collier and Steph were here because they were about to bust the place and I just about walked in on it. Now I'm sitting in the back of their car and there's no fucking door handles and I can't get out on my own or else I would have been on my way back an hour ago."

"Oh, my, god, Corey. Did you get arrested again?"

"No." Corey shook her head violently, though Thayer couldn't see it. "I didn't I swear. Protective custody more like, maybe."

"Are you okay?"

"Yeah, I'm fine," she breathed, relieved. "A little frustrated—a lot frustrated."

"Hmm. Are you alone?"

"Yes, for a while now." She craned her neck around and could just make out the top of Collier's head not far away as he gave commands to more officers. "I don't know how long I'm going to be. Please don't be angry."

"I'm not angry, sweetheart. Just disappointed."

"Why?" Corey sat up. "What did I miss?"

"Well, I've done my workout and my body is very warm and supple right now—and very sweaty. I can feel drops running down my neck and chest and between my breasts."

Corey groaned and slouched down in the hard bench seat, her knees banging into the back of the front seats. "Oh, babe, don't tell me things like that."

"Don't you want me to take your mind off your current situation? I read somewhere once that police cars are designed to be able to be cleaned easily, like taxis."

"Whoa, you are not suggesting what I think you are." Corey squirmed a little, her jeans feeling a little tighter.

"Not really. I'm not that kind of girl. I'll go outside to cool off."

"I think they're wrapping things up here. The parking lot has emptied quite a bit and even some of the police are leaving now."

"Do you want me to stay on the phone with you?"

"Yes, please." Corey sighed. "I'm really sorry, babe."

"As long as you're okay I'm..."

"Thayer?" Corey straightened on the seat.

"I heard something. I think someone is breaking into the shed. Probably kids or a raccoon or something. Hold on a sec."

"Thayer, go back in the house." Corey ordered across the line, her heart leaping into her throat when she got no reply. "Thayer, can you hear me? Get back in the house, now."

"Collier!" She shouted and banged on the glass. "Collier! Steph!" She pressed her face against the cage and closer to the open window. "Oh, god, I need help!"

"Calm down, Corey." Steph poked her head through the open driver's window. "What's wrong?"

Corey held up her phone in a shaking hand. "Thayer's in trouble." Her voice was trembling. "I think he's there."

"Collier, we need to go. Crandall's at Thayer's." Steph shouted and jumped behind the wheel. "If the connection is still live put it on speaker. Make sure it's on mute. Hold it up so we can hear it."

Collier, to his credit, didn't hesitate and got on his radio. "Warren, get down the lake in the boat—now. The suspect is at Thayer Reynolds's place. Consider him armed and dangerous with one hostage."

He didn't wait for a reply and slid into the car. "Go!" He turned to face Corey, concern and rage in his eyes as he pulled out his own phone and hit record in an attempt to capture what he could for evidence. "Hold your phone up."

Thayer stopped at the bottom of the deck stairs reconsidering her decision to investigate while barely dressed and barefoot. Even if it was an animal it could be sick or angry and kids causing trouble in the middle of the day seemed suspicious too, especially with the vandalism going on around town.

She raised the phone to her ear again as a tall, older man in khaki pants, fishing vest, and matching floppy hat came around from the back of the shed.

He smiled. "Good afternoon."

Thayer studied him, a prickle of fear skittering across her skin, taking in the thinning, shaggy hair, sharp features, and dimpled chin. She tensed in recognition and his narrowing eyes were all the warning she got that she was in danger. He was already moving when she turned and bolted back up the steps to the deck.

She made the mistake of looking back, which slowed her enough for his long reach to swipe at her legs as she hit the top of the stairs, gripping her bare ankle and sending her crashing forward onto the deck. She turned her head at the last instant, saving her from smashing her teeth out but the side of her face took the hit, stunning her. The phone shot out of her hand and came to rest a few feet away beneath a chair.

"Corey!" Thayer screamed as she scrambled toward it, tasting blood in her mouth. He was on her fast, pulling her back by the legs across the deck and bringing a knee down across her lower back, pinning her to the deck with his weight.

"Get off!" she shrieked and struggled to get out from under him.

"Settle down, young lady." He increased the pressure against her back and a large calloused hand wrapped around her neck from behind. "I don't want to hurt you."

Thayer gasped and panted against his weight, her heart hammering in fear. She rolled her eyes to the phone. She could see the time still ticking and knew the connection to Corey was still active. She stilled, gathering her strength. "What do you want?"

"That's better." He eased some of the pressure off her. "I need to get out of here. I had a good thing going here but because of my good-for-nothing nephew and his inability to exercise even a modicum of self-control, the police are looking for me. I expected to be gone before you realized I was ever here. I don't intend to hurt you but I will if you get in my way. With your cooperation I can get out of here quicker."

"What do you want?" Thayer asked again, sliding her arms even with her shoulders and placing her palms against the deck, ready to move as soon as she got the chance.

"I need fuel," he replied simply.

"Fuel?" Thayer wasn't sure she heard him correctly.

"Gas for my boat. It's anchored just up from your place, and I walked the woods along the shoreline to get here. I need fuel and one of your canoe paddles to navigate the outlet to the river. Then I will be away from here and you will be unharmed. Your shed is locked. I assume that's where you keep it."

"Yes." Thayer swallowed hard. "Okay. Take it."

"Good girl." He shifted his weight and removed his hand from her neck. "I'm afraid I can't let you go until I'm well away from this place, and I'm going to need you to remain here and not alert the police to my presence for a while. I will ensure you can free yourself without too much trouble."

Thayer craned her head and saw him unwinding line from a spool. "No. No. No." She jerked and thrashed until both his knees pressed into her back, forcing the air from her lungs.

"Calm down," he ordered, leaning heavily on her.

Thayer couldn't help a desperate sob. "You don't have to do this," she gasped, unable to take a full breath.

"I know who you are, Dr. Reynolds. I've met your grandmother a few times years ago and you when you were a child. I've researched my neighbors thoroughly before I set up shop here. I know you're a smart woman, and I also know you've recently had a life-threatening scare. I can't imagine you want to go through that again."

"No," Thayer grunted, the pressure on her growing.

"So, cooperate and I will be gone and you will be free in half an hour." He shifted his weight from her and straddled her back. "Put your arms behind your back."

Thayer took several gulping breaths, swallowing hard before bringing her arms behind her and crossing her wrists.

"This is twenty-pound test monofilament. You won't be able to break it, and trying will only injure you. Do you understand?"

Thayer choked back tears of fear and rage and helplessness as the thin line bit sharply into her skin as he tied her and she fought the urge to struggle. "I understand."

He moved off her entirely and Thayer risked a glance to her phone only a few feet away, the connection still showing. If Corey was listening, she knew the police would be on the way. If Corey was listening she would be going out of her mind with fear.

"Tell me the combination to the shed," he demanded.

She swallowed, her mouth desperately dry, her throat tight. "Um, fourteen, seven, seventeen."

"Fourteen, seven, seventeen," he repeated.

"Yes."

"I appreciate that you're probably in a fair amount of discomfort right now, but I would rather not worry about you, so I would ask that you remain exactly as you are. Do you understand?"

"Yes." Thayer swallowed trying to reconcile his articulate and polite speech with his brutality.

She released a shaky breath when she heard him leave the deck, his boots crunching across the yard back to the water line.

"Corey?" Thayer whispered as loud as she dared. So far he gave no indication he knew about the phone and she certainly didn't want to draw attention it. "It's Harold Crandall. He's here. He needs gas. He's getting away by boat. The police need to get someone on the lake and cover the launch points and the outlet."

She heard him walking across the yard and the banging against the aluminum canoe as he wrestled a paddle free from inside before his footsteps grew louder again nearing the shed and then nothing else for several, agonizing minutes.

"Son of a bitch!" He roared in fury and stomped back across the yard and up to the deck.

"Corey, I love you," Thayer whispered seconds before he reached down and hauled her to her feet by one arm.

Thayer cried out, the line cutting into the skin at her wrists, and wavered on her feet in front of him. "I said I didn't want to hurt you but that doesn't mean I won't." He spat at her. "What's the combination?"

"I told you." Thayer winced and leaned away from his fury. "Seven, fourteen, seventeen."

"That's not what you said." He glared at her, his eyes narrowing dangerously. "You playing me, girl?"

"No." Thayer shook her head. "I'm not. I'm scared. Maybe I misspoke."

He ground his teeth, gripping her hard around the upper arm, lifting her to her toes and marching her toward the stairs.

Thayer's shoulders ached with the added strain and her wrists were on fire. "You're hurting me."

"Should have thought of that earlier."

CHAPTER TWENTY-NINE

"Oh, God, what is that?" Corey groaned, rocking back and forth on the seat. "Twenty-pound test? What does that mean?"

"Fishing line," Collier answered through gritted teeth.

A strangled sound tore from her throat and her vision wavered.

"Hey!" Collier barked and banged on the metal separating them. "Curtis, look at me."

She struggled to focus and battle back the terror threatening to consume her. She felt like she couldn't take a full breath her fear was so acute.

"Corey. Take it easy. Stay with me."

She gasped a breath as if she'd been underwater and met his gaze. "Okay. I'm okay." She clawed her hands through her hair as they listened to the events unfold. "Oh, god, babe, tell him the right combination."

"That's not it?"

"She reversed two numbers. She's stalling him." Corey shook her head, hot tears spilling down her face as she listened to Thayer speak directly to her and heard the fear in her voice when Harold Crandall came back for her.

He looked at her intensely. "I swear to you, I will not let anything happen to her."

Corey nodded and swallowed hard. "Please, don't leave me in here."

"I won't." He shut off his phone as Steph pulled off to the side of the road twenty yards from the start of the driveway.

They exited the car, leaving the doors open and Collier opened the rear door for Corey to scramble out. "Do exactly as I say. Stay behind us and stay quiet. Are you with me?" He gave her a hard look.

She breathed deeply, fighting panic. "I'm good. I got it."

Steph drew her weapon and turned on the camera affixed to the center of her duty vest. "Can you see the shed from the side of the house?"

"Um..." Corey swallowed several times, "...no. If he's anywhere near the shed he won't see us."

Collier nodded toward the house and they moved down the driveway, staying low. Corey wanted to scream at their slow pace. They tucked up against the side of the house and stilled when they heard the clear sound of shuffling feet and Thayer's pained breathing.

"On the ground," Crandall snarled and they heard a rush of movement followed by Thayer crying out when she hit the ground. "On your belly."

Corey tensed, her muscles coiling to push off the wall, but Collier's forearm crossed her chest, pinning her back, his face all she could see.

"Stay still," he hissed. "We wait until he leaves her."

Corey nodded and he released her. He reached in his pocket and pressed something into her hand before moving away. She felt the cool hardness of the object and glanced down at the black, folding knife Collier had given her.

They waited another eternity while listening to Crandall wrestle with the lock and throw the shed doors open. He banged around inside for a few minutes and they were close enough to hear the sloshing of liquid in the gas can when he lifted it.

"There are pruning shears in a bucket by the door," he commented casually. "It won't be easy but you should be able to manage." His voice grew distant as he moved away, his steps crunching across the yard.

Collier communicated silently with Steph, raised his weapon and moved around the house as quietly as a man of his size could, Steph right behind him. Corey released a slow shaky breath before following.

Her heart hammered in her chest with relief and worry seeing Thayer already struggling to raise herself to sitting. She turned toward them, her face a mask of confusion at their sudden appearance.

"You did good, Doc." Collier's eyes flicked to her before returning his steely gaze toward the trampled path of vegetation Crandall made on his way through as Steph took up position on his other side. "Is he armed?"

"Jim?" Thayer stared at him.

"Does he have a weapon?"

"I don't...I didn't see..." she stammered, shuddering with each breath. "Corey?"

"I'm here." Corey dropped down behind her and flipped open the knife, her hands hovering shakily over Thayer's raw, swollen wrists. "Oh, shit, babe," Corey breathed, her throat tightening.

"Cor...Corey..." The shudder turned into violent full body trembling. "I can't feel...my hands."

"I know, babe. Don't move." Corey eased the blade between her wrists, careful not to do further damage. The blade was sharp but the line cut a furrow into her skin and Corey had to saw through eliciting an agonized sound from her before the line gave and her arms dropped forward.

"Oh, god," Thayer gasped, hunching in on herself as she brought her arms forward, resting her hands, palm up against her legs.

"Get her in the house, Curtis," Collier growled, his eye twitching wildly with his level of fury. He nodded to Steph and the two of them disappeared into the brush after Harold Crandall.

Corey knelt in front of Thayer. She was alarmingly pale, her tank sticking to her chest and back, dirt smeared across her sweaty skin. Corey cupped her hand around Thayer's neck, encouraging her to lift her head. "Thayer?" Corey bit down on a gasp at her bruised face and bloody, swollen lip. "Can you walk?"

Thayer blinked rapidly, tears coursing silently down her face, leaving tracks through the dirt on her cheeks. "I don't... um, I'm sorry..."

"It's okay. It's okay. I got you." Corey moved closer to her. "Put your arms around me." She shifted to one knee and slipped one arm around Thayer's back and the other under her legs. She could deadlift more than Thayer's weight on her worst day, and charged with adrenaline, she barely registered the effort it took to stand with her and adjust her in her arms.

She walked as smoothly as she could, trying not to jar her, as she moved up to the deck and back into the house and to the large overstuffed sofa.

Corey startled when Thayer's eyes closed to slits on a gasp of pain. "What?" Corey asked, panicked. "Thayer, what's wrong?"

She sucked in a breath, her body shaking hard and her hands twitching. "My hands." She worked to open and close her fingers. "Circulation and nervous function are returning."

Corey grabbed the throw blanket from the back of the sofa and shook it out before draping it over Thayer, placing her arms on top of it. "That's good, right?"

Thayer winced. "It hurts."

"Tell me what to do." She could manage without instruction but she hoped giving Thayer something to focus on, someone to treat, even if it was herself, would help her stay present.

Her body continued to spasm and tremble even as she tried to relax against the sofa. "Just a stress response," she murmured, closing her eyes. "Low blood sugar, dehydration, exhaustion..."

Corey moved through Thayer's house, knowing it like she did her own. She grabbed water and a high-calorie protein drink from the fridge. The first aid kit was under the kitchen sink. If one of them needed something that was not in it, they should probably be on their way to the hospital.

She dropped everything on the coffee table. Thayer's eyes were closed but Corey could tell she wasn't asleep by her uneven breathing and the tremors still wracking her body, her hands jerking as they recovered feeling and blood flow. She went back for a bowl of warm water, soap, a clean washcloth, and the bottle of pain meds she kept here.

Her third trip through the house involved collecting a couple of ice packs from the freezer and a clean towel from the bathroom. She froze and Thayer's eyes flew open as four sharp cracks echoed around the lake so fast they were hard to count. They both knew what they were.

"Corey?" Thayer's voice broke.

"It's okay." Corey assured her with more confidence than she felt as she sat down on the edge of the sofa. "Collier and Steph know what they're doing."

Thayer nodded and swallowed hard. "I know."

CHAPTER THIRTY

Corey slouched against the kitchen bar, elbows resting on the countertop. She was exhausted and shaky, her heart still beating hard from adrenaline and fear. The place was crawling with officers now and she watched through the window as Collier walked with the paramedics alongside the stretcher that held Harold Crandall handcuffed to the rail.

"How's she doing?" Steph asked, reaching for the fresh pot of coffee.

"She's hanging in, dozing off and on with the pain meds. The fishing line cut her but not too deep. She has full range of motion and feeling in her hands and fingers. Other than that just some bruises, and she refused to go to the hospital. Said it wasn't necessary."

Steph offered a smile. "Well, I guess she would know, huh?"

"I guess," Corey murmured, hanging her head.

"Hey." Steph reached across the counter and placed a hand on Corey's arm. "I've been on the force a long time and you wouldn't believe some of the shit I've seen. What Thayer went through today—what you went through—may not be as bad as it gets but it's pretty damn close. You are two of the most courageous people I have ever met. You'll get through this, okay?"

"Yeah, okay." Corey nodded, fighting tears. "Thank you."

Collier stepped into the house, wiping his feet before joining them in the kitchen. He nodded to the coffee. "That fresh?"

"Yeah." Steph reached for one of the mugs Corey had set by the coffeemaker.

"You don't have to do that." Collier jumped, his hand meeting Steph's over the mug and Corey couldn't help a small smile.

He cleared his throat and grabbed the mug. "I'm perfectly capable of making my own damn coffee."

"Of course." Steph stepped away, meeting Corey's eyes over her mug.

He poured his coffee and said, "Paramedics say his condition is serious but think Crandall should pull through."

"Guess I need to spend more time at the range," Steph muttered.

Corey stared at her, unsure if she was joking. "You missed?"

"She didn't," Collier answered. "Two rounds from ten yards out from both of us. All hits—just not fatal ones."

Corey simply nodded. "He was armed?"

"Internal Affairs frowns down at us shooting unarmed people."

Steph asked, "When do they want us to go in?"

"As soon as we're wrapped up here. Your body cam was on so it will be quick."

"Have you shot someone before?" Corey blurted, slamming her mouth closed with a click of teeth at Steph's troubled expression. "Sorry. None of my business."

"Today was a clean shoot, Austin," Collier rumbled. "Nothing to worry about."

Steph's expression relaxed. "Thank you, Sergeant."

Collier cleared his throat and gestured to the coffee and his already empty mug. He looked at Corey. "You mind?"

Corey waved him on. "Pour me one too."

Collier topped up his own and poured a mug for Corey. As soon as her fingers closed around the handle and took the small weight, a laser-like pain shot down the right side of her neck and shoulder, numbing her fingers. She hissed a breath, her hand going limp. The mug bounced once on the granite counter, spraying coffee before shattering pieces across the counter and floor.

"Fuck." She gripped the back of her neck with her left hand and backed into the dining room to avoid the mess.

"Corey?" Steph hurried around the bar. "Are you all right?"

"Curtis," Collier barked. "Where are your pills?"

"No. No." Corey shook her head and sagged against the dining room table. "I can't. It'll knock me out and Thayer needs me. It's just a muscle spasm."

"What can I do?' Steph asked with concern.

"It'll pass." Corey tried to find the source of the tension and work out the trigger with her left hand.

"Don't be stupid, Corey. You just said it yourself. You need to be there for Thayer." Steph pulled out a dining room chair and turned it around. "Straddle it."

Corey raised her brows and smirked despite the pain.

"You wish. You want to take your shirt off?"

"You wish." Corey lowered herself onto the chair and hung her arms over the back. She grunted, her back arching when Steph's hands dug into the spasming muscles in her shoulders and neck.

"Christ, girl, is this what it's like every time?" Steph winced.

"Mmm, this one isn't so bad." She dropped her head, the spasm beginning to ease. "When it morphs into a migraine, imagine a brain freeze that lasts hours not seconds."

"I'm sorry." Steph continued to work on her muscles. "Is this helping?"

"Very much." She sighed. "You could give Thayer a run for her money in the massage department."

Collier cleared his throat behind them, reminding her he was still there. "I'll just clean this up," he muttered.

Corey's shoulders shook with silent laughter seeing Collier crouched on the floor mopping up coffee and picking up shards of broken mug. "I think we're making him uncomfortable," she whispered to Steph.

"Good."

Before Corey could say more, the door banged open and one of the junior patrol officers walked in. She recognized him but couldn't remember his name. He was overweight, his uniform top straining around his waist. He was more than a little out of breath, his jowly face ruddy with exertion. His eyes darted around the room, widening when he saw Steph giving Corey a back massage. "Heard there was coffee. Didn't realize I'd get a show too."

Steph's hands stilled against Corey's back. "What the hell did you just say to me, Taggart?"

"Thought if there was going to be any girl on girl, the hot doctor would be involved at least. You'll do, Austin, but you cost me twenty bucks. I had you as straight in the pool."

"You want to say that again, Taggart?" Collier asked coolly as he stood from the other side of the counter and set down the rag and mug shards.

"Sergeant Collier," Taggart stammered. "I didn't, um...I was just..."

Collier moved around the counter to stand between the patrolman and his view of the living room. "In one pathetic, perverted breath, you have insulted and degraded my friends and my partner."

"I didn't...I meant no disrespect."

"Yes, you did. Those three women are stronger, smarter, and have more goddamn heart and grit than you could ever hope to possess. You will speak *to* them and *about* them—and every other woman on the goddamn planet—with respect. If I ever hear bullshit like that come out of your stupid face again, Taggart, I will personally see to it that you are on traffic control for the rest of your miserable, uninspired career. Do. You. Copy?"

"Yeah, yes, Sergeant." Officer Taggart's voice cracked nervously.

"Get out of my sight."

Taggart had probably never moved so fast in all his life as he disappeared back out the door. Collier reclaimed his coffee and resumed his position leaning against the counter. "Where were we?" he asked as he looked at them over his mug, his eyes flashing triumphantly.

Corey muttered, "Officer Austin, I'd like to report a murder."

CHAPTER THIRTY-ONE

"Corey, is something wrong?" Thayer asked drowsily when Corey joined her again on the sofa. "I heard Jim shouting."

"Nothing, babe. Collier and Steph are in the kitchen. They're handling it."

Thayer made an ineffectual move to pull herself up. "Do they need to speak with me?"

"Here." Corey grabbed a pillow and eased her forward slightly to place it behind her so she was sitting up more. "No, not today." She assessed Thayer carefully. Her color had returned and her trembling had ceased. She placed her hand on Thayer's chest over her heart.

Thayer sighed. "What are you doing?"

"Checking your vitals." Corey smiled gently.

"And?" She moved a hand from her lap to place over Corey's.

Corey's throat closed and her chest tightened again with all the fear and desperation of earlier. Her breath shuddered and her eyes filled with tears. "I love you," she whispered, tears falling silently onto their hands.

Thayer brushed tears from Corey's cheeks, her own eyes shining with emotion. "I was really scared."

Corey nodded. "More or less scared than last time?"

Thayer closed her eyes briefly. "How is that even a question we have to ask?"

Corey had no answer. It seemed so absurd that they were going through this again. The only difference being their roles were reversed, though she would take being physically injured any day over the sheer terror and emotional agony of knowing Thayer had been in danger.

Thayer moved the towel and ice packs from her lap and let them drop to the floor so she could pull Corey closer, cupping her hands around her face and brushing her tears away with her thumbs. "Would you believe me if I said I was equally afraid because all I could think about both times was never seeing you again?"

Corey gulped a breath somewhere between a sob and a laugh and dropped her head onto Thayer's chest, her emotions cracking open fully as she wept and clutched at Thayer's shoulders.

"Oh, sweetheart," Thayer whispered. "I'm okay." She ran her hands through Corey's hair and across her back, holding her close. "We're okay." She continued to hold her and murmur soothing words until Corey quieted. "You know, maybe we should look at this as a unique opportunity."

She raised her head, searching Thayer's golden eyes, dancing with love and humor. "For what?"

"Couples therapy." Her lips twitched into a smile.

"Seriously?" She gaped at her. "You're cracking jokes now?"

Thayer's smile widened. "Ouch." She touched her fingers to her split lip and tempered her smile. "I'll fall apart later. We'll never make it if we're both a wreck at the same time, so you let me know when you're ready to take over."

Corey almost came unglued again at Thayer's strength and humor, the love in her eyes and gentle smile on her lips. She was determined to keep it together. "I think you can safely tag out whenever you need to, babe. I got this."

"I know you do." She pulled her down for a tender kiss. "Can I ask you to help me with some things now?"

"Anything." Corey sat up.

"I would like to take a bath." Thayer started to push herself up. "And I'm starving and all I can think about right now is that pan of leftover lasagna."

Collier and Steph were waiting for her when Corey emerged from helping Thayer to the tub. She had filled it with water and bubbles and left Thayer alone at her request. Corey knew she needed time to process what had happened and was relieved she felt safe enough now to be alone.

"Everything all right?" Steph asked.

"Yeah." Corey flicked the oven on and got the pan of lasagna in one hand and a beer in the other. She slid the pan in the oven and cracked the beer, draining half at once.

"Are you sure?" Collier asked.

Corey wiped her mouth with the back of her hand. "Yeah, I'm sure."

"All right." He nodded. "We're heading downtown. We have to start the report, check in with the hospital and meet with IA and the brass about the shooting."

"You're leaving?" Corey glanced around for the first time and considered the house and yard through the windows. There were no more police, the coffee pot was empty, and there were half a dozen mugs in the sink. All her attention had been so thoroughly focused on Thayer that she really had no idea what had happened or what time it was.

"Yes, but we're leaving Warren here," Collier said. "He's outside in his car at the moment, but he'll be patrolling the property and checking the perimeter overnight, including any traffic on the lake."

She straightened, alarmed. "Why? Is something—"

"No." Steph held up her hand. "You and Thayer are safe. We just wanted to make sure you felt that way."

Corey blinked at her, her gaze darting to Collier, who wouldn't meet her eyes. He looked away, as if embarrassed at being caught out in an act of compassion. "Thank you."

"Try and stay out of trouble for Christ's sake. You two could probably find danger in a greenhouse. Think I'm getting an ulcer," he barked over his shoulder as he headed for the door.

Corey stared after him, feeling overwhelmingly grateful for his presence in her life, thinking maybe one day she would tell him—or maybe not.

"You two going to be okay?" Steph broke into her reverie.

"Um, yeah."

She reached out and squeezed Corey's hand. "Call for any reason, okay?"

"Thank you." She walked her to the door. She saw Warren sitting in his car in the middle of the driveway and she watched Steph and Collier speak to him a moment before they left.

Corey knocked softly on the bathroom door. "Thayer, you okay?"

"Yes."

"I'm going to grab a shower in the master. Just bang on the wall if you need anything."

"Mmm hmm."

She kept her shower short, just needing to scrub off the film of fear sweat she felt still clung to her. She toweled off her hair before slipping into clean sweats and a T-shirt. The kitchen and living room smelled of lasagna and Corey wished she were hungry, but the idea of eating held no joy for her. She pulled the pan from the oven. There was still no sign of Thayer.

"Thayer, the food is hot."

"Be out soon."

She didn't want to intrude on whatever Thayer was going through right now. Thayer knew she was here and where to find her. She pulled a plastic container from the cabinet and filled it with lasagna, sticking a fork in the middle of it. She grabbed a few napkins and a bottle of water and headed out to the driveway to feed Officer Warren.

She chatted with him for a while and found she liked him. He was a local with family in the area. He went to JCU for a degree in criminal justice and was six years out of the academy. He was ambitious to move up and was studying for the detective's exam already.

It was getting dark by the time Corey headed back into the house, and she was surprised not to find Thayer either in the kitchen or the dining table. The pan of lasagna was right where she had left it and was untouched, except for the piece for Officer Warren.

"Thayer?" The bathroom was dark, the air still warm and damp from the bath.

She stepped into the doorway of Thayer's bedroom, and though the light was off, she could see her wrapped in her thick white bathrobe, hair damp, lying on her side in the middle of the bed facing away from the door. "Babe, are you all right?"

The only answer Corey heard was a shuddering breath and anguished sob as Thayer's body began to shake before she finally broke down.

Corey crossed the room, slipping onto the bed behind her and gathering her close against her. "I'm here."

Thayer pulled them even closer as she cried. Corey had no idea how long they stayed like that. There were no words and Corey didn't offer any. She just held Thayer close for as long as she needed. Her breathing slowed and Corey thought she had fallen asleep until she stirred, gripping Corey's hand and slipping it inside her robe, placing it over her breast.

"Touch me," Thayer rasped, her voice hoarse with emotion.

Corey tensed, not pulling away but uncertain. "Thayer—"

"Please, make love to me. Help me forget just for a little while."

Corey pushed herself up on one arm and tugged gently on Thayer's shoulder to roll her onto her back. "Babe, are you sure?"

"Yes," she whispered, her golden eyes dark with distress and arousal. "This is what I need."

Corey held her gaze as she tugged the belt on Thayer's robe loose, parting it open and caressing her breasts and belly, her skin warm and smelling of lavender from the bath. She eased the robe from Thayer's shoulders and pulled it from beneath her, leaving her naked on the bed.

Thayer sighed, her lips parting slightly as she clutched at Corey's shoulders and let her eyes drift closed.

Corey knew she just needed to be loved gently and completely to be taken care of—caressed inside and out—until she felt safe again. Corey removed her hands only long enough to strip off her clothes before she lay next to Thayer, their naked bodies as close as she could get. She stroked her sides and back with long, slow sweeps of her fingers.

Thayer shivered beneath her touch, skin pebbling and nipples hardening with the stimulation. Corey reached for the blanket at the end of bed to cover them. Thayer wrapped her arms around Corey's waist and simply held on while Corey covered her with languid touches and soft kisses across her neck, chest, and shoulders. Without their usual playful banter, relentless teasing, and power plays, they were left with a quiet, intense intimacy where Corey poured out all her love and strength and Thayer opened herself up and let it fill her emotionally and physically.

Thayer's climax was as heartbreaking as it was beautiful, and Corey silently wept with her when she cried out. Her anguish and ecstasy seemed to drain completely, and she collapsed in Corey's arms.

She pulled Thayer close, tucking her head into the crook of her neck and pulling the blanket over them again. Sleep was a long time coming for her, but she was content to feel Thayer's warmth, heart thrumming close to her, and listen to her breathe, safe and peaceful.

CHAPTER THIRTY-TWO

Corey woke to streaming sunlight and an empty bed. She slid her arm over to Thayer's side, but the sheet was cold. "Thayer?" Corey rolled over, squinting out the window. The sun was bright and seemed well past dawn. She had slept late. "Thayer?"

For a moment she managed to forget the horrors of the day before, but then she blinked and they came rushing back in a flood of terror, forcing Corey to her feet and into her discarded clothes. She skidded down the hallway, panic racing through her heart as she pinballed off the wall and into the kitchen. "Thayer."

Thayer's head jerked up from her plate, her eyes wide with alarm as she pushed herself from the table to stand. "What's wro—"

Corey slammed into her, wrapping her arms around her in a fierce hug. "You weren't there."

"I'm sorry, sweetheart." Thayer sounded confused. "You were sleeping really hard and I was hungry."

She tightened her grip and buried her face in Thayer's neck. "Are you all right?" She pulled away but kept her arms laced around Thayer's waist.

"I'm okay, I promise." Thayer looked her over. "Are you?"

She ignored the question and grasped Thayer's hands in her own, wincing at the dark red abrasions circling her wrists.

"Corey," Thayer said sharply to get her attention. She pulled her hands from Corey's grasp. "I just needed to eat something."

She blinked a couple of times. "Right. Okay. Right." She looked around. "What are you having?"

"Lasagna."

"For breakfast?"

"More like brunch. It's nearly ten." Thayer shrugged. "Do you want any? You haven't eaten in a while."

"No, thank you." She felt out of sorts and out of balance still. "Just coffee."

"I made a pot," Thayer said as Corey shuffled toward it. "I wish you'd eat something."

"Later." Corey poured herself a mug. She stood at the counter drinking it when Thayer's hands came around her waist from behind.

"Thank you for taking care of me last night." Thayer kissed the back of her neck.

"You're welcome." She turned in her arms and circled Thayer's waist. "What else do you need?"

"I need you to take care of yourself too," she said seriously, before reaching across the counter to where Corey had tossed her glasses at some point. "Put these on. I need the light right now."

Corey slipped them on, realizing all the blinds were open where they'd been keeping the house dim for her. "Better."

Thayer nodded. "Pick something and eat, sweetheart, please. I need you strong because I don't know if I can be right now."

She breathed deeply, understanding. Thayer wouldn't be able to focus on herself if she was worrying about her.

Thayer kissed her gently before going back to her still warm heaping plate of lasagna.

Corey popped a bagel in the toaster and topped up her coffee. "Do we need to feed and water Warren?"

"He left twenty minutes ago."

Before Corey could comment, there was a knock at the door. Her eyes flicked to Thayer who went rigid. "It's okay. I got it." She felt a little jumpy too and was acutely aware for the first time that Thayer didn't have a peephole. She made a mental note to put one in. She stared at the door as if she could see through it.

"Corey? Thayer?" a familiar voice called. "It's Rachel."

"And Dana," a second voice chimed.

Corey exhaled and opened the door. "Hey." The sight of their friends with matching expressions of concern and relief nearly undid her again.

"Hey." Rachel saved her from having to say more by offering a powerful hug, which she gratefully returned while Dana scooted by them, giving Corey's arm a brief squeeze.

"I'm glad you're here, Rach," Corey said when Rachel finally let her go. She frowned at the gauze bandages around Rachel's arms and hands.

"I'm fine, dude. Gives me an excuse to see Frankie to touch up my vampire pinup girl," Rachel answered Corey's unspoken comment, referring to the tattoo artist they both saw. She gestured to the tattoo beneath her bandaged right forearm.

Corey nodded absently. "Wait. How did you know to come here?"

"Collier called the shop this morning and told me what happened, and he told me I should come out. I called Dana."

She moved from the door. "Come in."

"Holy shit this place is fucking amazing." Rachel looked around the kitchen and great room. Dana was sitting in a chair at the table opposite Thayer, applying ointment to her wrists.

Thayer seemed relaxed with her friend and Corey was grateful for their presence. "You want coffee?"

"Do I want coffee?" Rachel scoffed. "Hey, gorgeous, how are you?" She wrapped an arm around Thayer's shoulders and gave her a kiss on the cheek.

"Better now." Thayer leaned into her for a moment.

Corey poured them both a fresh cup. "Let's go outside."

She brushed her hand across Thayer's back as she went by and was rewarded with a loving smile. With Dana here she knew she was in good hands.

They stepped out onto the deck into the bright sunshine and warm late August air. Corey adjusted her glasses as she stared over the lake and tried to reconcile the peaceful beauty she always enjoyed with the horrifying violation they had endured not twenty-four hours before.

"You want to talk about it?"

Corey was quiet a long time, working to settle her emotions. "I thought I was going to lose her, Rach." She finally breathed. "In the most horrible way imaginable. My mind was going through every fucked-up thing he could..." her voice hitched, "...he could be doing to her and I was so far away."

"Don't, Cor. Don't torture yourself with what might have happened. You were here. The police got him and Thayer's okay."

She blinked back tears and toed the dirt at her feet, not even realizing she had walked down the deck and over to the shed where they found Thayer. Her foot hit something hard and she reached down to dig it out of the dirt. She stared dazedly at the knife Collier had given her.

Rachel sucked in a breath. "Was that his?"

"No." Corey brushed dirt off the blade and folded it closed. "It's the knife I used to cut Thayer free. He tied her up with fishing line."

"Motherfucker."

"Yeah." Corey closed her eyes tight against the image. "Let's go in."

Dana was at the table wolfing a plate of lasagna. "I never say no to Nana's lasagna," she mumbled.

Corey's eyes darted around. "Where's Thayer?"

"Getting dressed. The police called and asked her to come down to the station." She looked at Corey with concern. "Thayer told me everything. How are you doing?"

Corey took a moment to think about the truth of that. "I'm okay," she finally said. "I'm glad you're both here."

Rachel gripped her hand. "Get dressed and we'll head back into town with you."

"Yeah. Thanks."

"In the meantime Dana and I are going to do some damage to your leftovers." She headed to the kitchen.

"Plates are to the left of the sink," Dana called out as Corey headed to the bedroom, the normalness of the moment easing her tension.

Thayer was already in soft worn jeans and slipping on a long-sleeved T-shirt. Corey's eyes were drawn to the gauze bandages around her wrists.

She saw her looking and pulled the sleeves of her shirt down. "I don't want people to see."

Her voice was strong and clear but Corey heard the grief behind it. "I know, babe." And she did. The shame of being a victim, however misplaced, was real and brutal.

Thayer sat on the edge of the bed while Corey dressed in her own jeans and T-shirt. "Do you want kids, Corey?"

Corey's head popped through the neck of her shirt. "What?"

"I've never asked if you want to have a family—be a mom— because, I do. Not right now but soon, and we should know that about each other."

"Yeah, babe, I want kids—a couple, at least. I'm an only child so, you know, siblings would be cool. You know, maybe a dog first." Corey was relieved to be able to answer her honestly but she worried about Thayer's casual way of discussing something so significant, especially at the moment.

"Yeah, a dog would be nice. This place deserves a dog. Will you stay here with me, then?"

Corey buckled her belt before dropping to her knees in front of Thayer. "For as long as you want." She ran her hands over Thayer's legs.

"Forever?" Her golden eyes were piercing in their intensity. "I want forever, Corey."

She sat back on her heels and sucked in a breath. "What are you asking?"

"I'm asking you to move in with me."

Corey's mouth opened but no words came out.

"I know it's soon and crazy and before you think it, I can tell you this is not the trauma talking. I've wanted this—wanted you, wanted us—from the first moment you undressed me with your eyes in the morgue."

Corey snorted a laugh. "That's romantic."

"I'm not asking you to give up your independence. I don't want that either. I have a life outside of us too. I'm not even asking you to give up your condo. Just maybe move the things over that are important to you so this can be as much your home as it is mine, and we can see how it goes. I want you to be my partner not my girlfriend—to cook dinner with me, to relocate your movie collection and your posters. To mow my lawn— our lawn—and help weed the garden when you have time. And other things not chore related. I want to make decisions about our future together." Thayer took a breath. "Do you want that too?"

Corey looked away, her mind spinning with arguments of too soon, U-Haul memes, and lesbian bed death horror stories. But over the din of her doubts all she could hear was the one word screaming from her heart—yes. "Can we get a lawn tractor?"

Thayer smiled, eyes dancing. "And a dog."

CHAPTER THIRTY-THREE

Officer Warren was waiting for them at the desk when Corey and Thayer walked into the station, hand in hand. They hadn't spoken much, each lost in her own thoughts but taking comfort from the other's nearness.

"Good morning, Dr. Reynolds, Ms. Curtis." He nodded to each of them politely and handed them each a visitor's pass. "I'll take you up." The door buzzed open as soon as he had his hand on it.

The room was alive with the lights and sounds of police work, but Corey knew she was not imagining it when the din quieted in a wave as they walked through. Her eyes flicked to Thayer, walking tall and confidently. Thayer's hand tightened in hers, and Corey knew she was reacting to the looks—some with admiration, some with sympathy and some with curiosity.

They traversed the entire room to the back offices and Warren knocked sharply on Lieutenant Williams's closed door before pushing it open. She rose from behind her desk and

Collier and Steph stood from the two chairs on the opposite side. All eyes were on Corey and Thayer, full of concern, but no one spoke for a beat, perhaps unsure what to say.

"I'm okay," Thayer announced into the strained silence. "We both are." She raised her hands, wiggling her fingers to emphasize her words. "My career as a concert pianist is not in jeopardy."

Lieutenant Williams smiled appreciatively at her humor. She gestured to the vacated chairs in front of her desk. "Please, Dr. Reynolds, Ms. Curtis, have a seat."

Corey waited for Thayer to sit before taking the other chair and moving it closer to her before sitting. She idly wondered if she thought it was Thayer who needed the closeness or if it was she who needed reassurance. It probably didn't matter and they both benefited.

"Thank you both for coming down," Lieutenant Williams began, not returning to her chair but perching casually against the edge of her desk in front of them. "I hope we can get you in and out of here quickly and back to some normalcy in your lives."

"Beginning to think this is normal," Corey muttered, pressing her lips together in silence when Thayer shot her a disapproving look. She could see from the corner of her eye Steph suppressing a grin and Collier rolling his eyes.

Lieutenant Williams, if she heard, chose to ignore Corey's snark and pressed on. "The hospital has been keeping us updated regarding Harold Crandall, and though critically injured, he is expected to make a full recovery. We have made a series of arrests with regard to the distribution of methamphetamine in this city." Her eyes flashed to Corey. "But that you're already aware of, of course."

Corey inhaled deeply and offered an apologetic smile. "Yeah, sorry about that."

"Well, while your presence at our operation was unexpected and troubling, it did open a door to an opportunity we don't normally have." She turned her attention to Thayer. "Dr.

Reynolds, you're aware of the active connection from your phone to Ms. Curtis's?" At Thayer's nod she went on. "What you may not know is Sergeant Collier recorded the entire…"

"Assault," Thayer supplied.

"Yes, your assault."

Corey stiffened in her chair, apparently the only one with a problem with the direction the conversation was taking.

"The quality is not the best, but we were able to reduce background noise and clean it up to make it clearer, and we will certainly be able to use it as evidence in bringing charges against Crandall for assault and forcible confinement, for starters."

Thayer nodded. "I'm grateful, I guess, that something positive will come from something so…" she sighed, her eyes closing, briefly, "…harrowing."

Lieutenant Williams's expression turned grim. "I'm sorry to have to ask you this, but I'm hoping you will agree to listen to the recording and let us know if there was something said that could help us strengthen our case, something that didn't get picked up by the phone."

Corey's eyes jerked to Thayer, who visibly paled at the request. Her own heart thudded painfully in her chest at the thought of listening to Thayer being afraid and in pain. It wasn't her decision, and she clenched her jaw so hard, in an effort not to speak, she thought her teeth might break.

"We have time," Lieutenant Williams held up a hand. "We don't have to do this now."

"No." Thayer inhaled deeply. "It's not going to get easier with time, and if there is something, I'm more likely to remember it now. Play it."

"I don't want to hurt you."

Harold Crandall's voice filled the room from Lieutenant Williams's laptop, the recording starting right after he had initially subdued her.

Thayer sucked in a breath and leaned forward in her chair, resting her elbows on her knees and steepling her hands over her mouth as she listened to her own ragged breathing and terror-laden voice.

She closed her eyes as the recording continued and concentrated on removing herself from the emotions of yesterday and keeping herself present in the room today. It was over and she was unhurt. Harold Crandall, when he recovered, would be going to prison and Robert Crandall was already in hell. She could listen to this without reliving it and provide them with the information they needed. She was strong, she was safe, she wasn't alone, and she could do this.

"Oh, god, what is that? Twenty-pound test what does that mean?"

The faraway sound of Corey's voice coming through the recording did nothing to diminish the fear and agony Thayer heard, and she sat straight up in her chair, eyes flying open. It hadn't occurred to her that she would hear the other end of the connection, and hearing Corey's naked desperation was like a knife turning in her gut.

Corey sat frozen in her chair, staring at nothing, her hands gripping the arms so tightly the skin of her fingers blanched. Her whole body was so powerfully tense it looked as if she might shatter.

"Stop," Thayer commanded. "Stop the recording." She turned to Corey and pried her hand from the arm of the chair, gripping it hard in one hand. "Corey, look at me, please." She reached to the back of Corey's neck feeling her muscles like stone under her hand.

She turned, meeting Thayer's gaze, and her distress was a living thing. Thayer knew her expression was a mirror of what she must have looked like the night Corey was brought in by ambulance, unconscious and fighting to breathe.

"Corey," Thayer said strongly and squeezed the back of her neck to encourage the muscles to loosen. "Please try to relax, sweetheart."

"I'm okay," Corey insisted, nodding her head and swallowing hard. "It's fine. I'm fine."

Thayer frowned at her, knowing she was lying. Everyone in the room knew she was lying. "Go ahead." Corey looked to Lieutenant Williams. "Play it to the end."

Thayer nodded in agreement. This time as she listened, she focused on Corey, not taking her eyes or hands off her and trying to ease some of the tension from her neck.

Lieutenant Williams closed her laptop at the end of the recording after Harold Crandall grabbed Thayer from the deck and dragged her over to the shed and away from the phone. She looked intensely at Thayer and Corey in turn. "Thank you for doing that. I find it hard to listen to it, so I can't even imagine what you must feel."

Thayer sat back in her chair, closing her eyes and pressing her fingertips against her temples while she collected herself. "That's actually a pretty good quality recording in my opinion."

"Almost like you can imagine it happening," Corey deadpanned and reached for her hand.

"Stop it," Thayer admonished halfheartedly as she laced their fingers together, just happy that she could make a joke, however dark.

"Is there anything you want to add?" Lieutenant Williams asked. "Anything that he said that we can't hear?"

"No." She shook her head. "What you have is… comprehensive."

"Okay. Thank you." Lieutenant Williams returned to her chair on the other side of the desk. "Sergeant Collier, would you like to fill them in on the rest?"

Now that some of the pressure was off, Corey felt some of her tension easing. She blew out a quiet breath and turned her attention to Collier.

He cleared his throat and straightened from the windowsill he had been leaning against. "We got DNA results back from Dr. Marsh this morning. Not that there was any question at this point, but the body is Robert Crandall. We also received results from the tox screen on the hair."

"And?" Thayer asked.

"And, I'm sure it will come as no surprise, but it showed a long history of drug abuse."

"So, cause of death?" Corey asked.

Collier shrugged. "Unknown but drug related for near certain. Given the fact he was found naked underneath his house, it may be fair to assume he was suffering some sort of psychotic break. Whether that's what killed him as opposed to simple dehydration, we'll never know. In any case, the investigation into his death is closed."

"You say that like there's a part that isn't closed," Corey commented. She was pretty much way past caring about the skeleton, but she wanted to know how the story ends.

"We've been following up with some cold cases with unmatched DNA available and we've had three hits so far."

Corey straightened. "You were right."

He nodded. "They were all unsolved sexual assaults. Two in Oneonta and one here. The matches are just partials, but we're going to have the lab guys look at it all again and the investigating officers go back over the evidence with an eye toward Robert Crandall."

Corey shook her head. "Jesus Christ."

"We obviously can't bring him to justice but we will be able to offer some closure and perhaps, peace of mind to these women. It's early days and Officer Warren is still checking into cases. There may still be more, probably are."

"I'm not sure whether to hope there are or there aren't more," Thayer commented.

"I'm with you there, Doc," Collier agreed. "In any case, you two are free to go. Did my best to keep your names out of the press and I think it may have worked this time. There are so many witnesses from the bait shop who are tripping over each other for their ten minutes of fame that the press hasn't pushed for too much about you."

Thayer smiled. "Thank you but I won't hold my breath."

"We better go see Lil," Corey suggested.

"Right." Thayer groaned. "Ugh. What's the opposite of 'third time's a charm'?"

Lieutenant Williams walked them to the door of her office and while Steph lingered with them, Collier ducked behind them toward his desk. "Thank you both for coming down and for all you have contributed…" She took a breath, "…and sacrificed to help us build our case."

Thayer nodded. "We're glad we were able to help."

"Please, don't hesitate to call if there's anything we can do to support you, and I would be happy to provide some recommendations for some great people who could help you through this if you need to talk."

Thayer breathed a laugh. "Thank you but I have a therapist I intend to call—again." She glanced at Corey. "Since I met Corey I've had to become an expert at mental health self-care."

Lieutenant Williams arched an amused brow looking between them.

Corey frowned. "Wow, Thayer, that stings."

"Sorry, sweetheart." Thayer reached for her hand. "That didn't come out like I intended. I just mean I never expected my life in Jackson City to be so fraught with danger."

Corey groaned. "Not really selling this whole moving in together thing right now."

Thayer laughed. "I'm sorry. I'm sorry. I'll shut up now."

Steph grinned. "You guys are moving in together?"

"It's been proposed." Corey pursed her lips and eyed Thayer.

"And accepted." Thayer smiled at her adoringly and squeezed her hand.

"Hmm," Corey grunted but her eyes shone with love.

"I'll walk you out." Steph gestured toward the exit.

Corey raised Thayer's hand and kissed the back. "I'll catch up." She gestured vaguely in the direction of Collier's desk.

"Sure." Thayer nodded before joining Steph.

Collier was bent over his keyboard, tapping away and Corey was shocked, given his love for a pen and notebook that he could type. She dug in her pocket and held out her hand.

"Found this in the yard this morning and wanted to make sure you got it back."

He looked up at her and then to the knife she held out to him. He pushed himself to his feet and leaned back against his desk so they were closer to the same height. "Keep it."

Corey looked at the knife and back to him, puzzled.

"So, you can remember."

She laughed humorlessly. "You think I could forget?"

He studied her for a long moment before he closed her hand around the knife gently and covered her hand with his own. "To remember how badass you are."

Corey stared at his hand over hers before meeting his eyes, feeling the last of her anger toward him fall away. "I never forget that either." She grinned cockily but jammed the knife back in her pocket. He snorted a laugh and she decided to run with it. "You know, um, I understand the police academy accepts applicants as old as thirty-six. Was thinking you could write me a recommendation."

Collier stiffened, his face draining of color.

Corey fought a laugh. "I kinda got a taste for all this detecting—" She froze when Collier clutched his left arm, his face contorting in pain as he slumped against his desk with a groan. "Collier! Oh, shit." She reached for him and looked around wildly for Thayer, her heart leaping to her throat. "Hang on, oh, Jesus."

He relaxed his face and straightened up and Corey stared, blinking at him in confusion as he broke into a shit-eating grin.

She sucked in a sharp breath, her hand going to her chest, her heart still pounding. "You fucking bastard."

He threw his head back and roared a laugh. "Yeah, well, you had it coming with that stunt, Curtis. The academy—you are so full of shit."

Corey tried to stay pissed but he was so happy about his joke she had a hard time keeping a straight face. "Just remember when your fat ass does finally keel over you're going to end up on my table."

"And that very thought is what's going to keep me alive for a very long time until I die peacefully in my sleep of natural causes."

She shook her head, her smile sobering. "Thank you, Collier." She blew out a breath. "For being there for Thayer—and for me."

"Yeah, well, you know."

"Yeah, I know."

CHAPTER THIRTY-FOUR

"Where are you going?" Corey called when Thayer immediately disappeared down the hall into the bedroom after they got back from seeing her grandmother. They had explained what happened and assured her they were okay and not to worry if she heard anything on the news.

"Getting ready for work," Thayer called back. "I've got the dreaded two to midnight swing shift this week. I really hate this shift. It's so hard to adjust to these hours."

"Work?" She leaned against the doorframe as Thayer kicked out of her clothes. "You're not going to work."

Thayer's eyes met hers. "I beg your pardon?"

She cleared her throat. "I mean, you need to give yourself some time, Thayer."

Thayer smiled softly. "Corey, I love you and I understand better than anyone how worried you are, but please don't tell me what I need."

"Thayer—"

"I need to work, Corey." Thayer scanned her closet pulling clothes off hangers. "I need to help people by doing what I'm good at. A job that empowers me, and most of the time fills me with confidence and a sense of self-worth," she explained while getting dressed.

Corey had no argument for that and was aware that any objection she could offer had more to do with her own fears than Thayer's needs. "I'm sorry," she said softly.

Thayer looked up at that. "For what, sweetheart?"

"I don't know." Corey shrugged. "For not being more supportive. For feeling afraid when you're so strong and—"

"Hold it." Thayer closed the distance between them. "You are allowed to feel whatever you need. Don't you dare apologize for that—especially to me." She waited for Corey's nod of understanding. "And really I'm taking my cues from you and how you handled things two months ago."

Corey's eyes widened in panic. "You're sending me away?"

"What?" Thayer looked puzzled. "No, sweetheart, of course not. I just asked you to move in with me."

"Oh." She breathed. "Okay."

"I mean, I'm doing what I need and not catering to other people's desires or perceptions of how I should feel or behave. Not even yours."

"But I was wrong then."

"I disagree. Everything that happened then led us to where we are today, and today, with a few notable exceptions, is pretty damn close to perfect. So how could I wish it had gone differently?"

Corey sighed deeply. "I understand. You're right."

Thayer leaned up to kiss her softly on the lips. "I usually am."

"What am I gonna do, then?"

"Here's a wacky thought," Thayer called as she moved into the bathroom. "Wouldn't it be weird if you worked at the hospital too, and went in to work, like one does on workdays?

Then, if you were feeling anxious or edgy you could just pop up for a quick visit."

Corey laughed and flopped down on the bed on her back. "Two cars or one?"

"Two unless you want to hang around until one in the morning."

For the first time since Thayer had been working at JCMH, there was no one waiting to be seen and she ducked into the doctors' lounge. It was after eight and she regretted not taking a break earlier as she scanned the fridge to find it empty but for a half-eaten yogurt with the spoon sticking out, a sandwich with someone's name tagged on it and a bottle of water. She grabbed the water and her bag of supplies from the locker room and sat on the sofa, laying everything out on the coffee table.

It had been steady but not slammed. Still she felt wrung out and shaky. She dug in the bag for the small scissors, intending to treat her wrists and change the bandages. Her dexterity and strength were normal but her wrists burned like she had been holding them over a fire, and she wanted some more ointment to help with the pain and speed healing.

Her hand shook as she tried to hold the scissors steady, her snips awkward and ineffectual causing her to sigh in frustration

"It's not a life-saving measure," Watson Gregory said quietly from behind her, "but I can help you with that if you'd like, Dr. Reynolds."

Thayer jumped, startled, her head whipping around. "I didn't realize you were on tonight."

"I'm picking up some hours I owe back in trade."

She nodded. "Thank you, but I can manage." She tried again with the scissors and failed.

"Here." He moved around and scooted the table back to sit on it in front of her. "Let me."

She sighed, resting her forearms on her knees. "Thank you."

He quickly snipped through the gauze wrapping and scanned the thin, angry abrasions, gently turning her hands over to see the extent.

"What? No crack about how I like it rough?" Thayer said bitingly.

"What? No, um, I'm—"

"I'm sorry," Thayer replied wearily. "That was a shitty thing to say."

He was quiet a long time. "It's okay. I deserve that."

"No, you don't."

He studied her injuries again as he uncapped the topical analgesia. "What happened?"

"You don't know?" she asked, surprised. Collier had told them he kept their names out of the press but she hadn't really believed him.

"I got the impression there was some new hot gossip but no one talks to me."

She smiled grimly. "There was a big arrest out at Rankins Lake—"

"That I know." He cut her off while gently dabbing ointment around her wrists. "It was all over the news. The police busted the bait shop for selling meth and arrested the supplier when he assaulted a woman who lived—" He stilled, looking up slowly. "That was you?"

"Yes."

He studied her hard, and he appeared to focus on her split lip and the dusky bruise across her cheek not quite covered with concealer. He frowned and looked back at her wrists brushing his fingers lightly over the abrasions. "I'm sorry that happened to you. Should you be working? I can pick up some of your shifts."

"Thank you," she said sincerely. "I'm okay."

"You're shaking."

"I haven't eaten and the fridge is pretty bare."

"Oh. Wait." He pulled a sandwich still wrapped in cellophane from his coat pocket. It looked like it had seen better days. "It's from today, I swear. I grabbed it earlier but ended up sneaking away to the caf for hamburger mac 'n' cheese Monday." He offered an embarrassed smile. "I can't remember if it's tuna or egg salad," he babbled as he unwrapped it and set it on the table. "But, um, you're welcome to it."

Thayer eyed the misshapen sandwich but something about his childlike generosity tugged at her. That and she was really hungry. "Thank you." She picked up half and started on it as he rebandaged the wrist he was working on. It was egg salad.

"How did it happen?" He began on the other wrist and Thayer switched hands to eat the other half of the sandwich.

"Um, I was in the wrong place at the wrong time, I guess. Which is particularly distressing because I was at my own house."

Dr. Gregory assessed her face again. "He hit you?"

"No. I was running away and he knocked my feet out from under me and I fell on the deck. Then he said some really articulate and conversational yet threatening and terrifying things while he tied me up with fishing line."

He sucked in a sharp breath, her battered wrist in his hand. "Jesus Christ."

"It wasn't for long," she went on. "The police and Corey were already on the way. I was on the phone with her when it happened, and the connection was still active so she knew I was in trouble. They got there pretty quick."

"You seem pretty casual about it for someone who was just terrorized in their own home."

She drew a deep breath. "I guess I hope the more I talk about it the easier it will be to accept and deal with."

"Well, shit," he said as he taped off the gauze around her wrist. "You're a stronger woman than I am." He immediately blushed and cleared his throat.

"Yes, well, I imagine I'm more of a woman than you in pretty much all ways." She crammed the last of the sandwich in her mouth as she gathered up her things. "Thank you for your help Dr. Gregory—and for the sandwich."

"Um, Dr. Reynolds? Did you mean what you said to me the other night?"

Thayer turned and arched a brow at him. "Every word."

"I mean the part about believing I could be a good doctor."

"I meant every word, Dr. Gregory."

Corey straightened from the wall as the door banged open. They hadn't heard her when she cracked the door a few minutes ago, and while her first instinct was to go in guns blazing when she saw them together, she was glad she chose to slip back out and hover by the door.

Watson Gregory stiffened visibly when he saw her and she tried to keep herself relaxed offering what she hoped was, if not an open, at least not openly hostile expression.

He stared at her a moment before giving a brief nod and hurrying away.

Good enough. Corey pushed the door open to the lounge just as Thayer emerged from the locker room.

"Hi." Thayer smiled, her eyes lighting up.

"Hey." Corey looked her over. "You okay?"

"I am, yes." She cocked her head. "Are you just leaving now?"

"Yeah." She ran her hands through her hair. "The morgue is a shit show of paperwork fuck-ups and a pileup of undisposed amputated limbs. There's a body that should have been out of there days ago, and at least two death certificates that have bounced back from vital records. Fucking amateurs."

Thayer laughed and slipped her hands around Corey's waist. "That's why you make the big bucks."

"That's the last time I let Webster let someone else loose down there."

"Where are you going to be?" Thayer asked, looking up at her.

"I'm going to pack up some stuff in my truck from my condo."

Thayer's eyes flashed. "So, I'll see you back at my place?"

"No." Corey grinned crookedly. "I'll see you at home."

EPILOGUE

"What time is the party?" Thayer called from the bathroom.

"Uh, I think it started at seven and goes until whenever." Corey slipped into her dark jeans and buckled her belt.

"So, we're already an hour late is what you're saying?"

"Don't worry about it." Her voice was muffled as she pulled her shirt on. "It's at a cop bar. There will be people in and out all night long. No one will notice or care what time we get there." She finger-combed her still damp hair and debated gelling it slightly to get it to behave but decided not to interrupt Thayer in the bathroom.

"What's this place like that we're going?"

"I've never been," Corey answered. "It's a bar called the Black Oak, a block from the station, so naturally, cop bar."

"So, casual?"

"Did you miss the part where I said cop bar?" Corey laced up her boots.

"I just don't want to stand out."

"Ha! That's funny." Corey spoke to the closed bathroom door. "Hate to break it to you, babe, but the only way you're not standing out is if we don't go at all."

She checked herself in the mirror one last time. She was fine in dark jeans and a burgundy, fitted, V-neck shirt. "When in doubt go black. That's all I got."

"That's what I was thinking. Is this okay?" Thayer asked from behind her.

Corey spun and took in Thayer's calf-length, black, long-sleeved shirtdress. On the rack or anyone else it would be modest and casual, but Thayer looked as glamorous as she would in a ball gown and twice as sexy. Her auburn hair was down in careless curls around her face. She accentuated her look with simple gold earrings and thin choker. "Wow." Corey looked her over from head to toe and back again, a slow smile lighting her face. "You look fantastic."

Thayer returned her smile and her gaze as she crossed the room to smooth her hands down Corey's chest and across her belly, slipping her hands beneath her shirt to feel her tight abs flex at her touch. "You look pretty hot yourself."

She sucked in a breath. "Don't do that unless you don't want to go," she warned and gripped Thayer's wrists to still her explorations.

Thayer smiled slyly and removed her hands. "Sorry."

"No you're not."

"You're right." She grabbed her purse and headed to the door. "We better leave before I change my mind."

Corey patted her pockets to make sure she had everything and followed.

The bar was full and loud and getting fuller and louder by the minute by the time Corey and Thayer got there. It was dim and swarming with off-duty and uniformed police officers making it moderately intimidating.

"Holy shit. There you two are," Rachel blurted, appearing in front of them from the crowd. "Thought you were going to leave me hanging. I don't know anyone here."

"Rachel?" Corey frowned. "What are you doing here?"

"Are you kidding?" Rachel frowned back at her. "Collier and Steph come into the shop like twice a week now. She was in the day she opened her promotion letter. I probably was the first one to know." She leaned over to a bemused Thayer and kissed her on the cheek. "Hi, gorgeous. You look sensational."

Rachel was rarely seen in anything but workout clothes and her work uniform of cargo shorts or pants and T-shirt. Tonight she had on black jeans, gray T-shirt, and dark gray, fitted blazer with the sleeves pushed up displaying a handful of tattoos crisscrossed with the thin, pink scars from the glass injuries. Her hair was artfully punked out and she was wearing silver hoop earrings.

Thayer looked her over and gave her a sultry smile. "So do you, Rachel."

"Hey." Corey scowled at their flirting glance. "Standing right here."

"Anyway, don't you and Collier ever talk?" Rachel asked.

"You mean like on the phone?" Corey snorted. "I don't even talk to you on the phone. No, we don't talk unless there's a case between us and it's been quiet." Corey shrugged and glanced to Thayer. "I haven't seen him since, you know, everything."

"Well, he asks about you all the time and it's starting to creep me out." Rachel rolled her eyes. "He bugged me all week about whether you were coming tonight, so you better make time to talk to him."

"Sure." Corey was puzzled. "I mean, I was going to."

"All right, enough about you." Rachel dismissed Corey and grabbed Thayer by the hand, pulling her farther into the bar. "In hopeful anticipation of your impending arrival, I ordered drinks and scored us a table."

"Sounds perfect." Thayer followed.

"Not you, dude." Rachel nodded at Corey as she made to follow them. "I totally drank your beer while I was waiting. Can you go to the bar for another round?"

Corey glared at her, in jest. "You suck."

Corey fought her way to the bar, using her elbows and height until she was belly up but both bartenders were down at the opposite end. "Shit." She scowled at how many people with money out were between her and her beer.

"I got it," Collier said from behind her and let out a sharp whistle, grabbing the attention of one of the bartenders and a bouncy, busty young woman came right over. "Hey, Gina. Sorry about the whistle."

"It's cool, but only 'cause it's you, Jimmy." She snapped her gum in his direction and flashed him a smile. "Whaddaya need?"

He nodded toward Corey. "Whatever my friend, Curtis, here wants. Just put it on my tab."

Corey arched an amused brow at him and placed her order for as many beers and glasses of wine she thought she could carry.

He scowled at her. "Jesus, how many people did you bring?"

"I don't want to have to hassle at the bar every time." Corey grinned. "It's called economy of motion."

Gina piled up her drinks and Corey used every finger on both hands collecting them. "Thanks, Collier, you're a peach."

"Wait. Are you coming back?"

"I can do it all in one trip."

"I mean." He cleared his throat. "Will you come back?"

She paused at his expectant expression. "Yeah, sure." She nodded and disappeared across the room.

By the time Corey wended her way through the bar, greeting a few people she knew, their table was full with Thayer, Rachel, Kelly Warren and Steph. Lieutenant Williams was setting down a tray of shots in front of them. There was barely enough room now for the drinks Corey brought. "Looks like we're taking a cab."

Steph jumped from her chair and pulled Corey into a hug as soon as her hands were free. "Corey." She grinned. "I'm so glad you could come. It's good to see you."

Corey returned her hug. "Congratulations, Detective Austin." Corey picked up two of the shots and handed one to Steph. "Allow me to buy you a drink." She threw Charlene Williams a cheeky wink, which was rewarded with a laugh.

Steph clinked their glasses together and they tossed them back in unison. Corey sucked in a breath and nodded in appreciation to Lieutenant Williams for buying the good stuff.

"Only the best for the detectives in my division." She smiled. "It's good to see you two looking well," she added with a glance at Thayer.

"Thank you," Corey said. "Thanks to Collier and Detective Austin." She punched Steph in the arm gently. "Narcotics, man, that's great."

Steph nodded and snatched two beers off the table handing Corey one. "It was my first choice. I think this isn't the first or last time we'll see drugs running through JC like that, and I want to be on the front lines."

Corey took a long pull of her beer. "Was it your work on the Crandall case that finally got your promotion?"

"That and a glowing recommendation from the sergeant."

"Oh, really?" Corey arched a brow. "Now you won't be riding with him or in his chain of command, right?"

"That's right."

"So, does that mean there's room for—"

"Shut it." Steph cut her off. "Have you seen him by the way? I know he's been looking for you."

"Yeah, he's—" Corey winced. "Oh, shit, I told him I was coming back." She quickly glanced to Thayer to see her, Rachel, and Kelly Warren working their way through the shot tray. Looks like they were going to be here for a while.

"You're at a packed bar by yourself." Corey slid a beer in front of him.

He grunted his thanks and sucked down half of it. "I spend all day with these bozos. Don't need to pal around with them too."

"So, Steph's going to narcotics. Are you happy about that?"

"I don't like partners. And she earned it."

She eyed him and drank her beer. "You know I can almost guarantee she wouldn't be at all offended if you asked her out."

His eyes shot to her but he didn't speak for a long time. "What's it to you?"

She shrugged. "Nothing, I guess. Just thought I detected some chemistry." He looked thoughtful and had no snarky comeback so she left it at that. "I should get back."

"Wait." He put a hand on her arm.

Corey turned back to him, curious.

He cleared his throat a couple of times and set his beer on the bar before reaching into his shirt collar to pull out a small gold medallion on a gold chain. "St. Michael. Patron saint of police officers. A lot of guys wear it."

"I didn't know you were Catholic."

"My ex-wife was." He shrugged. "Some of it stuck and in my line of work, it's not like you can ever have too much backup."

Corey cocked her head wondering where he was going with this. "Yeah, I get it."

He reached into his pocket, pulling out a silver chain with a small silver medallion and held out his hand. "I got you one too."

She stared at it, confused. "St. Michael?"

"No. Take it."

She scooped it out of his hand and held it up, but there wasn't enough light to read the inscription around the half-inch silver oval.

"It's St. Teresa of Avila, a sixteenth century Spanish woman known for not giving a shit about other people's expectations and never letting anyone hold her back and tell her what she could and couldn't do—or what was proper." He snorted. "Course for her that meant committing herself to a life of devotion and piety, but you get my meaning. She was also a fan of pop culture, whatever that means, five hundred years ago."

Corey was positively stunned at the gift and her expression must have said as much.

"You don't have to wear it or anything, and I don't know what you believe but you know…" He seemed to have run out of words.

"You're not always going to be around to save my ass?"

"Something like that."

"Well, organized religion and I haven't ever been close, what with my lifestyle of mortal sin and all, but I have faith. You know, I see so many dead bodies I have to believe there's more to death than ending up on a steel table under my knife." She was thoughtful for a moment. "So, yeah, I believe in a higher power. It's a she, by the way."

"Obviously."

Corey unclasped the chain and hooked it around her neck, the medallion falling to the neckline of her shirt. She touched it. "She sounds badass. What's she the saint of? Fucking up the patriarchy?"

"Oh, yeah, that." Collier finished his beer. "St. Teresa is the patron saint of headaches."

Corey's head snapped up, her mouth agape. "You're shitting me."

"Look it up."

"Come on. There's a patron saint of headaches?"

"There's a saint for every goddamn thing you can think of." He waved at Gina behind the bar and held up two fingers. She promptly deposited two beers in front of them.

Corey grabbed one and took several long swallows to mask her whirlwind of emotions. "I don't know what to say." She held the medallion between her fingers, her eyes pricking with tears.

"You don't have to say anything," he said quietly, and Corey could see his own emotions behind his eyes. "Anyway…" He cleared his throat. "I like you better at a loss for words and you probably want to get back." He nodded across the room.

"Yeah. Will you come with me? You know, pal around for a while?" She grinned crookedly. "We're a hell of a lot better looking than most of the other bozos."

Collier rumbled a laugh. "Why the hell not?"

"Maybe I'll become a saint one day," she suggested as they crossed the crowded room.

"Sure, as soon as churches stop catching on fire when you get too close."

"You're so clever."

"St. Curtis, patron saint of 'inappropriate sarcasm' or 'public displays of idiocy.' No wait, I got it—patron saint of 'sad sexual encounters.'"

"Ha! I fucking dare you to ask Thayer about the last one. She's had a lot to drink. I'll show you. The church is gonna love me."

Bella Books, Inc.

Women. Books. Even Better Together.

P.O. Box 10543
Tallahassee, FL 32302

Phone: 800-729-4992
www.bellabooks.com

CPSIA information can be obtained
at www.ICGtesting.com
Printed in the USA
LVHW042013141219
640521LV00001B/2/P

9 781642 471021